Guillaume Dustan is the pseudonym of a high-ranking French judge in Australasia. *In My Room* was first published in France in 1996.

'Guillaume Dustan is the toughest new writer to emerge in a land known for its incorrigibles (Sade, Céline, Genet, Guibert). He explains nothing, he apologises for nothing – he merely exults in an evil that has become so banal that the *poète maudit* has turned into a *romancier sans sentiments*.'

– Edmund White

GW00459336

IN MY ROOM

Guillaume Dustan

Translated by Brad Rumph

Library of Congress Catalog Card Number: 97-81175

A CIP catalogue record for this book is obtainable from the British Library on request

The right of Guillaume Dustan to be identified as author of this work has been asserted by him in accordance with the Copyright, Design and Patents Act 1988

First published as *Dans ma chambre* in 1996 by
P.O.L. éditeur

Copyright © 1996 by P.O.L. éditeur

Translation copyright © 1998 by Brad Rumph

This edition first published 1998 by
Serpent's Tail, 4 Blackstock Mews, London N4
Website: www.serpentstail.com

Phototypeset in 10½/14pt Garamond by Intype London Ltd
Printed in Great Britain by Mackays of Chatham plc

10 9 8 7 6 5 4 3 2 1

CONTENTS

PART ONE

PART TWO

PART ONE

1 GOOD INTENTIONS

I left Quentin the bedroom. I moved into the little room in the back of the flat so I wouldn't hear them fucking. A few days later, a week maybe, I thought it was getting too sleazy. I demanded my room back. Of course Quentin immediately decided to move himself and Nico into the living-room, which meant I would have to bang on the wall to get them to quiet down the nights I had to go to work the next day. As a bonus I was also able to hear Quentin saying he was going to kick my ass and Nico replying Chéri, calm down.

I was living day to day, not knowing where I was going. It was not unpleasant. I'm always bored shitless whenever nothing's going on. This is no doubt why I was still living with Quentin even though we were no longer together. His most recent brainwave consisted of entering my room without warning. The first time I was lying on the bed jerking off, smoking a joint. The door opened. He advanced into the room. He said You wouldn't have found my mother's appointment book by any chance? She thinks she left it here. I didn't answer

the question. I said Knock before entering please. He
said I did knock. I said I didn't hear anything. He began
asking for his blasted thing again. I said Quentin Beat it
right now. He looked stunned. And then he went out.
It took me ten minutes before I was able to jerk off
again properly.

The second time he knocked. The instant I yelled No!
he entered the room. This time I was definitely getting
poked on the edge of the bed. I said Get out! He gave
me a particularly distraught look instead. I was mad with
rage. I said to the other guy Don't stop, he'll get out,
he's just doing this to piss me off. I focused on the
fucking. Quentin watched us doing it. He left in a while
without saying anything.

After that I decided I'd let myself get pushed around
no more. I started yelling systematically every time he'd
do something shitty to me. I'd yell about the cans of
food he hadn't replaced, about the disgusting bathroom,
about messages he hadn't relayed. I would insult him.
He would say nothing. I savoured my vengeance. I liked
being able to yell at him with impunity. Alessandro, a
great buddy of mine, was living there in the little
bedroom, so that put me at ease. I thought that in the
presence of a third party Quentin would not dare do
anything seriously stupid, he liked his comfort too much
to have to spend time in jail. And then one day I was
feeling pretty good and I started talking to him like
before. I talked about what I'd done the night before
with some hot guy. At the end he looked at me and said
You like that pretty little head of yours, don't you? Well

you won't be so proud of it after I throw acid on it. This dampened my enthusiasm. I asked Alessandro if he would agree to share a place with me. I didn't want to live alone. He said OK. As soon as I told Quentin I was going to move he began threatening me again. I asked Alessandro to start seeing his girlfriend at the apartment. And then it got to be so unliveable I ended up moving in with Terrier, into his rotten studio way up in the eighteenth arrondissement.

We were fucking better and better, Terrier and I. I had the impression I was doing him some good. I was the first person he'd told he was HIV positive. Needless to say, he had found this out the first time he'd been treated, when he was twenty, seven years earlier. Since admitting this to me he was no longer having nightmares where they'd nail down his coffin over him and he'd push on it with all his might but it wouldn't come open, and that's when he'd wake up. I had also restyled his look. I forced him to cut the bangs hiding his face and also the nails he was wearing long. It made him a lot better looking. A little less timid maybe.

I didn't want to move out of the neighbourhood. I found another place three blocks away. That was lucky. I was a little nervous at the idea of running into Quentin, but it was in a part of the neighbourhood we'd hardly ever go, and we didn't keep the same hours anyway. I left him all the appliances and the furniture we'd bought together. I had money however. I bought everything new at Darty one morning with Terrier. A new life was beginning.

2 ENCOUNTER

With Terrier it was hell. He'd get bombed. He'd make scenes in bars as soon as I would look at somebody. I realised he would not be able to change quick enough. I told him I'd see him only during the week from now on. The weekends I needed for me. I went out alone. The first night I had some guy who was no big deal. The second night I went to the Keller. First I got fucked a little by two guys in the backroom, then I came back and drank a beer at the bar. I got a grip again. I was getting a little paranoid from my look. I was afraid my light brown cowboy boots looked too tacky with my black leather 501s. Happily the top part looked all right: bare chest, black leather vest.

I saw right in front of me this guy leaning back, his elbows against the bar. It's his look that held me. I thought he looked absolutely normal, not at all the look of a guy playing the pervy tough leather type. Plus he was cute and had a nice body, was short and was obviously older than me. The look he was giving me was neutral. Then I ran into Serge. We'd fucked six years earlier at the time I'd just met Quentin (and at Quentin's no less, who was away on vacation). I asked him What about that one? He told me For a night it's very nice. And he's very well hung. This worked my nerves. I thought that now the guy had seen me talking with Serge, he'd know I knew he had a big one. This would make it more difficult to cruise him.

I went and stood next to him at the bar without looking at him. I waited a bit, not wanting to appear too obvious. Actually he was with another guy, a tall blond all in leather, kind of cute, who was laughing all the time. And then they weren't talking any more. My neighbour looked straight ahead, and then a little to his right. I took the opportunity and said Hi. Then I said nothing else, to appear butch. He said Hi. I said I'm Guillaume. He said I'm Stéphane. I said The guy you're with, is he your boyfriend? He said No, just a friend. I said Is he good sex? He said Yes, why, you want to meet him? I said Uh yeah. He said Eric, this is Guillaume. I said I don't know what just to feed the conversation. And than a big ugly sort in leather came up to our group and it was cool, he started hitting on me about doing pictures of me. I gave him my number, said I'd agree to a narcissistic session any time, and then I was rather negative on the art theme. I said that I didn't give a shit about art. The big society prick asked me And so what interests you then? What interests me is the fuck of the century I said, looking at Stéphane. It worked. I still had my oars to row, but I ended up bringing him home.

Serge was right in a way. The first time was nice, in

a kind of mad dog way. I liked what I was seeing in the mirror as he was fucking me front to front. I thought we looked good together. His great big dick hurt me a little but I sensed the potential. I decided to keep him. Instead of letting him get away I asked him if he was hungry. The fridge was full, I'd gone shopping that day. We ate in the kitchen.

I told him I thought he was real hot. He stiffened up, but not as if he was used to this sort of compliment, more as if he thought I was making fun of him. I told him It's not because you have one eye smaller than the other, that you have one that's green and the other one blue, and that you have one eyelid higher than the other that I'm going to stop thinking you're real hot if I think you're real hot. This surprised him. He softened up. I told myself I liked him. I gave him my number. I waited for him to call.

3 COUNTRY

It wasn't long in coming. We talked. In a while I said You know it pissed me off you saw me talking about you with Serge the other night because I thought you'd know I knew about your big dick and I thought you must have thought it was too obvious hooking up with you for that. He said it was true, guys were only interested in him for his dick.

Therefore I proposed we see each other for lunch rather than a fuck date. He arrived a little late. He was all in a bother, dressed pretty bad. I had chosen a chic place to impress him. Lunch went smoothly. I was not bored at all. We made a date to fuck again at my place since his lover was at their place. On that date, I wanked our cocks together, rock hard, mine 7×5½, his 9×6, I had to stop myself from getting hypnotised by it, I wanted there to be only two dicks, no difference, each one loving the other's as much as his own, no more no less. I also learned an item about his life history, his couple with Jean-Marc going downhill. They've been together for ten years, but less and less so for five, they haven't

slept together for almost two. Jean-Marc is at his boyfriend's this very moment. Stéphane tells me He's told
me he's in love with him.

We see each other a third time, a fourth time, a fifth
time. Each time he fucks me. But we talk also. We go
out walking. We're getting to know each other. I ask
him to talk to me about his life with Jean-Marc, and he
tells me as I expected that he spends his time doing the
shopping, the cooking, the dishes, and waiting for Jean-
Marc to fuck him. I tell him he shouldn't allow himself
to be treated this way.

We begin seeing each other on a regular basis. One
night a weekend, plus one night a week. Stéphane tells
me he doesn't feel he's really betraying Jean-Marc since
Jean-Marc is occupied on his side too. But it works my
nerves. I demand three nights a week. We eventually
start seeing each other every weekend, except the
nights they have a dinner at their place. The second
thing that's beginning to irritate me is I don't have the
right to fuck him because of the pact he has with Jean-
Marc. They each have the right to fuck anybody they
please, but not to get fucked. I point out to Stéphane
that from what he's told me this is not so fair as it seems,
since Jean-Marc doesn't like getting fucked anyway. I say
that it can't go on for long this way.

He asks Jean-Marc's permission. Jean-Marc doesn't
give, but he says he knows we'll go ahead without it
anyway. I invest. I take Stéphane to the country for the
weekend, to an ugly enough château-hôtel filled with
business people. Stéphane's a little uptight, he says he

doesn't usually do this sort of thing. I tell myself it's a little class hang-up of his he'll get over.

It's sunny in the suite. We take whirlpool baths. I've brought along packets of algae I saved from my seawater therapy. Champagne and joints when we wake. I nuzzle the head of my dick gently against his hole. I fuck him later, after the pool or a walk in the countryside, I don't know any more. I squeeze my thighs, standing at the edge of the bed. I'm a little limp because his ass is extra tight. I hate that, but all right, it's only starters. I'm very careful not to hurt him. He comes without touching his dick. He tells me it's the third time in his life. I wonder how many times it's happened to me before. It's true, it's not an everyday thing.

We come home Sunday night. Stéphane brings me back to my place before he goes home to their place. It's eight o'clock, a little early for the Palace. I lie on the bed. I smoke a joint, listening to music. I think about what Quentin asked me on the phone the day before yesterday. Do you still have the desire? I said Yes. And then I told him I cannot live with you. But tonight I tell myself that I really am going to be able to stop loving him because there really is someone else. I cry from happiness, I think that I will really be able to love him, that what I'm feeling is true, I wanna make you mine, I'll love you till the end of time, and it's such a relief. I tell myself it's a long time since I've cried for myself. I feel like calling Stéphane right now and telling him he must choose between Jean-Marc and me. He must decide this second. If he's not here in an hour I'll never see him again. And then I tell myself that wouldn't be so smart. I know very well he's going to leave him anyway. It's only a matter of time. But it gives me a weird feeling all the same. I stayed alone only two months. Well, not exactly. And all of a sudden I have an attack of paranoia, it has to be the hash, when I hear the tick-tock of the clock at the very end of the song by D:ream, it doesn't have at all the same effect on me as it did the first time I noticed it, when Stéphane and I were taking a rest after fucking. This time I tell myself it is the countdown to my finish. I'm afraid. I cry. And then I calm down and I'm able to make it to the bathroom, grabbing on to the walls I'm so blown away, and I'm still listening to D:ream while I take a shower trying to make the joint go away.

4 MY BOYFRIENDS

It's a century I haven't been out dancing. Stéphane doesn't much like to because he doesn't know how, but it makes him happy to make me happy so he's OK with it. We can't go to the Queen because I don't want to run into Terrier, but tonight there's a thing at the Bataclan, so after a few beers in a bar we go. At the Bataclan the music is just so-so and since the place isn't packed the ambience is cold, people are pretentious because it's a special soirée and at any rate there are too many heteros. In short, after an hour, when the effects of the gin and peppermint start to wear off, the Queen has become inevitable.

When Terrier sees me, my head is less than three inches from Stéphane. I'm asking him if he's found anybody for a three-way while I was off taking a piss. He tells me he didn't have the time. He smiles as he tells me this. Terrier is a deathly pale. He passes me by without a word.

I catch up with him in the toilets. I tell him Hey I knew it was you. He's a total mess. He says But who are

you? You know perfectly well who I am, I say. OK, and
so what are you fucking doing here, can't you leave me
the fuck in peace? he says. I say I have every right to be
here, shit. The fuck I'm going to hide out at home just
because you go out. And so he starts crying. You didn't
even recognise me . . . I wasn't thinking about you . . .
and there you were, with all that hair on your body . . .

I don't know what to do so I cut out. I grab Stéphane
along the way and drag him across the crowd. Past the
bar there's some space. I dance. It's Tony Di Bart.
Quentin had Nico bring it back from London for me last
December, three or four months ago, about the time I
met Terrier. I dance like a wild man. I toss my head
every which way, I feel my cheeks throb, I'm having a
hard time keeping my balance, a hole hollows out
around me on the floor giving me room. When I stop,
a guy I've frustrated shoves me in the back. The other
gorgeous wrecks, with shirts and muscles strictly over
the top, are all smiles. I'm out of breath, I look at
Stéphane, I start dancing again in a cooler fashion. I lift
my head. Terrier's ten feet off. Apparently following us.
I tell Stéphane Come on let's go upstairs. We go upstairs.
We smoke a cigarette, watching the dance floor below.
The music's good. I've got a buzz going, the gin and
peppermint and joints. I dance by the security barrier.
I rub up against Stéphane's ass. It gets me hard. We kiss.

When I open my eyes Terrier is there again at the end
of the gangway. He doesn't even pretend not to be
watching. I'm over this, I say. Let's get out of here. On
the way up the stairs and out I see at least five cute guys

I could do. But who gives a shit, I tell myself. I've already fucked a thousand guys in my life. The one I'm going home with is in the Top 4. So there.

And then outside Terrier shows up dead drunk. He is shirtless, just wearing a white tank top, black jeans, his white, slightly too thin shoulders shining in the night. To me he looks extra fucking hot. It's freezing cold out here. I'm coming home with you two, he says. You can't be serious, I say. Yeah yeah, it's gonna be great, he replies. I adore his drunken voice. It's not going to be great because you're not coming, I say. Oh yeah, and how're you going to stop me? he asks. Watch, I say. I catch him by the shoulder. I pivot him around towards the entry. Now! Go back in there! He breaks loose. He starts walking towards the Etoile. I follow. He starts running. I run. He speeds up. I'm getting excited. I finally catch up with him in the next block. OK now enough of this shit. You leave us the fuck alone, I say. He laughs at me. We head back down the deserted Champs-Elysées. I pull him by the wrist. You're hurting me, he says. I don't fucking care, I say.

There's a line to get in. I jerk him through the crowd to the door. The shame, the shame of it all, he's saying. The bouncer asks Sandrine, the girl at the door, These gentlemen? You know them? She knows him, I say, and he's going to catch cold. I let him get dragged into the entrance of the club. I think he'll be all right because of the remark he made before he disappeared into the haze, the persuasive house music. Maybe just one last drink? I go back to Stéphane. I'm definitely sobered up.

This definitely sobered me up, I tell him. I can see, he says. He's been waiting for me sitting on the hood of a car, real cute in his little green bomber jacket. Want to go to the Transfert, I say?

We finally decide not to bring anybody back home, and to fuck just the two of us. We go home. Four o'clock, MC Solaar on the radio, we enter the tunnel under the Place de la Concorde, the Quai du Louvre, the black cabby and his North African buddy are cool schmoozing. I tell Stéphane it's all right, it was just too much for me that's all. Terrier stopped there dead in his tracks on the way into the toilets, the first time he saw me with his replacement. It wasn't planned this way.

Five o'clock. Stéphane is on top of me. I have both my ankles on his shoulders. He's ready to enter. I don't want you to fuck me, I say. Oh yeah, he says? I want you to make love to me, I say. He says OK. The first fifteen minutes are perfection, my dick is out of its mind, hard without me touching it. I spread my legs to the max and take his nine inches. After a while it gets so good it reminds me of Quentin the way he fucks me so deep. I've got the hard-on of death. We come almost at the same time. After, he tells me he's beginning to understand what fucking is all about. I tell him that out of the thousand men I've fucked, there are four or five, OK a dozen, who know how to do what he has done to me. There is also Chad Douglas, but he's exclusively on cassette. In fact, he's listed on the credits of one of the ones I bought the other day, Remote Control. I only hope that in real life he's not dead.

5 SEX

Robert cuts me on the nape shaving me with a new blade. Do me a favour, I tell him, and put on some of this and wait a half-hour OK? That's how long you have to wait for the antiseptic to work, according to the label, for HIV. For the other diseases it's shorter. He says Thirty? I say Yeah. He says What if I just throw it out? I say Yeah. Robert likes me, he bought me coffee the time before, and today he offered me a Marlboro. Good-looking, straight, western look, big belt, worn 501s, wears bangs. I see him bending over the banister looking at me when I'm almost down at the bottom.

After this incident I was so uncomfortable I went somewhere else for a month. When I came back he was there. What's up? he asked me. Not much, I said. He did a trick I didn't know, a slow wink.

We leave Robert's salon. Stéphane walks behind me as usual. We go across the street to buy me a new bomber jacket and a pair of chaps. Chaps. For years I've been dreaming of chaps. I'm feeling rustproof. My hair is very short, I have on my black leather 501s, stormtrooper boots, a blue truck-driver sweater, the collar of my shirt adds just a dash of colour. I have seven years going to the gym behind me. A bit of a belly, just a bit, it goes away in two weeks if I do my abs. The only thing is my calves, a little on the skinny side.

Saturday at around six Stéphane came in from running an errand. He fucked me, it was nice, but I don't remember any of it. We had dinner. Alessandro made us pasta with asparagus, then he left for the Beaubourg he said, though in reality to see his GF. We do some more coke, with a joint. Stéphane is constipated. It works my nerves. I think he's still afraid of getting fucked. I say that, but it's true he has made progress. He told me that before, he only opened up when he was high on poppers. I send him off to shit and wash his ass. During this time, I take my jeans off, I put my boots back on first, then my super leather chaps. When he comes back, the latex chaps are open on the bed. The Rangers that fit him, and matching socks, are at the foot of the bed. I help him dress, and then I get him into place, knees on bed, ass in the air. I have trouble getting hard at first, seeing the real lack in preliminaries here. I look at his ass, I add some gel. That finally turns me on. I enter, not ripping hard, he's tight, so I open him up with the aid of the riding crop, my left hand holding him by the belt of his chaps, my right hand uses the crop on him, gently, on his bottom, his thighs, on the small of his back. I expand inside his ass, he clings to me, I turn around and what I see in the mirror is world class, it pleases me, it reassures me, it flatters me. I ram him a while, and then I'm sick of the position. I move him up on the bed, then we come back down to the edge, then I come out and I tell him to get in front of me, I've gone a little limp. I re-enter, I expand again in the condom. In the end he comes.

It's already two. I'm not up for going out. We're hungry, I open a can of tripe, make some ten-minute rice, two individual packets. There's some leftover Sancerre in the fridge. The tripe doesn't have much of a taste because of the coke. I put on Soft Cell. I bought two old albums I didn't know about except for the top hit song, Numbers. Who's that person you woke up next to today? Marc Almond asks me. I roll a joint and then I light it and then I turn off the stereo with the remote for the stereo and after that I turn on the TV with the remote for the TV because I haven't figured out yet how to put them both on the remote control I bought last week, and I search for something on cable and I pass the joint to Stéphane.

I'd like to put on Microdots, Cosmic Evolution, it's a great cut on the DJ Brainwasher CD, but the CD refuses the program. I look around for something repetitive but not cold to take a dildo by. It's five a.m., Stéphane's getting tired, he's falling asleep, but he told me it was OK to wake him for the dildo. I get out another compilation, Guerrilla in dub, the sixth cut must be appropriate if the title is any indication: Intoxication. Yes, it's fine. The bass is muted and cool. From time to time there are even some lyrics, a voice whispering Funky marijuana. I don't even notice this until I'm on my third dildo, the big black one. We began with the day-glo ultra-soft pink one I bought at the Pleasure Chest in West Hollywood two years ago when I'd gone away between hospitalisations. It's perfect for easing open an ass. Then another pink one, more imposing, the Kong ($9\frac{1}{2} \times 7$). Now the big black double-header bought in Berlin that is seven and a half inches around. I take it half-way. Off to the side is the enormous pink one, eight and a half inches around. I never take this one because it only goes in when I'm completely wasted. So tonight, with the quarter hit of acid, the coke and all the joints I've been smoking, I will be able to get it in and I know a pretty royal sensation is awaiting me, every bit as mind-blowing as a parachute jump or deep-sea diving. I like my sensations strong.

Stéphane smears it with gel. The black one is still in me because I prefer not to leave my ass empty too long, I have a hard time maintaining my erection if there's nothing left in when my ass is already pretty dilated. Stéphane adds gel to the big pink one, I insist on it drippy, if not, I feel it too much going in. Shall we? It goes in, first the head, fat as a fist, it forces the entry in one swoop, and then the one two three folds of flesh the cretins who designed the thing must have thought they were smart putting on the backside of it, I guess they thought it looked prettier that way. Wait, this hurts. It won't go in, I say, Take-it-out take-it-out take-it-out! Thirty-second break before trying again. OK there, it goes in, but it's still really big, it hurts me a little, even on a good hit of poppers. I wonder what I can do to

get turned back on and then I have an idea. I tell Stéphane Put you hand around it so I can feel how big it
is, that'll turn me on. It's apparently the turn-on of death
to feel from the outside just how much this enormous
fucker happens to dilate this hungry bitch ass of mine.
I get the only erection. I'm starting to get off. OK now,
fuck me with it. He does. I realise how fucking deep
he's got it in me, I've never had it so deep. Twenty
seconds mega-ramming and I feel ready to come. Pull it
out quick quick quick! He whisks it out. I explode. I
think about Quentin because he's the one who taught
me to pull out the dildo before you come. That way you
don't damage the sphincters. If the dildo is left in, the
muscles bang up against the latex and can't close back
during ejaculation. I check. As usual, as it's been for a
year now, not a trace of blood. This I learned on my
own. For exercises of this kind, if it hurts don't force it,
or you might end up bursting the blood vessels, and
winding up with a bleeding ass is no fun at all.

The day after is Sunday. We get up too late to do the
morning markets so we don't do anything. I roll a joint
after breakfast, we watch a little TV and then, since I'm
beginning to get bored, I decide to go down on his dick.
I suck on it a little while, and then I get up and go wash
out my ass in the bathroom. I give no explanation for
the noises he can hear. It takes me a while, and when I
come back I'm not turned on as much so I roll another
joint, we smoke it watching TV and then I go back down
on his dick and when he's real hard I get on my back
and I spread my legs and he gets on top and pokes me

deep, with a perfect comprehension of my entrails, my dick is rock hard without my touching, twenty minutes I think, I fondle him, I squeeze his tits, I press my expanding dick up against his abs, he does a trick I love doing too, he rolls his abs against my balls fucking me. Multiplication of the sensitive points. He tells me he wants to come, I say OK, a bump from behind and off we go. Penetration from behind is deeper and makes it easier for me to wank. I turn around, forty-five seconds we grope and then it's fine, he's settled in, I am around him, my crotch is heavy and gorged with blood, I wank, he rams me, I come before he does, afterward I cannot go on, he has to stop. I'm a little pissed he didn't come in my ass but he's happy anyway, he tells me it's wild to feel his cock like that in an ass. I know, I say, but I'm still totally on the ceiling. It's the first time I've managed to let his super-revved-up engine ram me so hard. I feel too spent to help him come right now. I tell him he'll come when I fuck him in a little while, OK?

Which is what happens an hour later. I have my spirits back now, we've been watching TV, I fondle him, my dick won't quit, my balls down at my knees. A tiptop, relentless, absolute erection. He doesn't know if his ass is dirty. He goes to shit and then to wash. When he comes back, I've gone limp. I spend a minute in his mouth to take care of that first. I slip into my condom. I put him on his back, a pillow under his head. I slide two fingers in him like butter. I go at it. Shit. Impossible to get in, he's so tight. I try again. Still no. I go limp. He looks freaked. I say All right, we're going to take our time. I place my ass on the bed, I nuzzle the head of my dick against his hole a good while, he relaxes, I get in extra-carefully. It's OK. And then I fuck him like I never have until now. It lasts a long time, the way I like. I see in his eyes he's beginning to take me seriously. I take him from the front, holding him first by the ankles. Then by the buns. Then by the middle of the thighs. Then where the knee bends. Then around the neck. I come back out to put on some gel. I re-enter. In the end he explodes. I come out, I pull off the condom, I jerk off looking at his ass, I think about the straight video I have called Juicy Anus. Its slogan is Any blown-open anus will be hosed down with big spurts of semen. Too bad we can't do that for real. I'm coming. I get back up. Boom. It's the fifth time we've fucked this weekend.

It's eleven. We go to dinner, totally wasted, nearby in the ghetto. The waiters are nice. A girl comes in from the Privilege, it was the anniversary of Tea Dance this Sunday. We're the last to leave the restaurant. It's cold in the streets. We are going to go to sleep together, three nights in a row for the first time. It's good.

6 AMERICA

I jerked off watching Eric Manchester pack in the action, doing what he knows how to do, tricks I know how to do. He's no Chad Douglas, but he loves his cock as much. I go brush my teeth, the nightly hygienic rounds: AZT, teeth, warts. I'll jerk off again maybe, I hope so, after all this. I see me in the mirror and I consider myself handsome. A slight, low-angle shot, then I choose other angles. I change expression, I have a look of concern, I tell myself my conception of beauty has changed. Before, I paid attention only to the shape of the body, the way it was put together. He could look stupid or tortured, he would still look good. Now, I tell myself the expression alone is beautiful. This is why I'm having so much success these days. I have the expression I had when I was fifteen, when I was away on vacation in Los Angeles at the Ls and people in restaurants would serve me alcohol because I was French even though it was prohibited for anyone under eighteen. Whatever I would do with the Ls was great, like drinking chilled California white wine in place of cranberry juice out of a cranberry juice bottle, in a cooler at the beach, the Pacific rolling in front of us. The smell of eucalyptus is very strong when we go down the hill to the beach. And it's chic, we're in a white Jaguar that did the twenty-four hour of Le Mans in 1964. Julie L takes me to dinner in Tijuana. We both order a talk-to-me-sideways, a steak with garlic and onion. The stylish Mexican ladies go to dinner in red or black evening gowns, the men in black suits. I have on a jacket Papa gave me that was too tight for him, and a blue oxford short-sleeve shirt with mother-of-pearl buttons which suits me very well because of my tan. I have on OP shorts, cream-coloured, in ribbed velvet. Marine-blue Docksiders. Cool. A Mexican sitting on the ground says Is he her son or her lover? as we pass by on the sidewalk of Tijuana's main street, around five or six in the evening, in mid-July. My father refuses to let me spend the following year with the Ls even though I could have gone to school at the Lycée Français which is just nearby.

It's been four years now that I've been thinking I am to die the next. I think I still look handsome though. I'm listening to Depeche Mode, In Your Room – higher love adrenaline mix, François Kevorkian's mix is the greatest.

I think about Quentin and me in LA two years ago. On arrival I announce to the Ls that the trip has been cut short. I'm allowed only fifteen days, the time for my platelets to go back down under twenty thousand. After that there's a serious risk of internal haemorrhaging, you have to go on the drip to bring them back up, and that can't be done here because it would cost too much. The Ls leave us after two days, they have to go away. As soon as we're by ourselves we start the usual fighting again. He says the usual horrible things to me, but not so horrible that we kill each other. I leave and go shopping at the supermarket, I calm down in the car. In any case it was inescapable. At the supermarket since it's late I find myself almost alone in the aisles of cans and packages. I buy everything you need to be happy. The heads of lettuce look like cabbage. There isn't any real cheese, only soft white with chives, for salmon. I spend time choosing wine, red and white. Pinot Noir. Chardonnay. From what valley? I read the geographic maps on the backs of the bottles. I go home. It's already the dead of night. I park in the flowers. I have the shopping bags in my hands when he appears on the threshold of the kitchen. He is not like he usually is. I realise he's not going to punish me.

I don't know why he agreed to making all this possible. The dense mist in the night on Santa Monica Boulevard, West Hollywood. The men come forth two by two, they're all dressed in the same tight T-shirts, very short jean cut-offs, thick white socks rolled down, combat boots. We dance to En Vogue, everybody knows the words, at a bar opened like a hangar on to the street, everybody knows how to dance. We go on to a back street to smoke a joint. I have a hard time breathing because of the humidity, but it's nice, him and me indestructible in the night in West Hollywood.

Probe. Spike. The Arena. A different place at the end of the world every night. We go shopping. At the Pleasure Chest some butch lesbians are ordering chains while I examine the kilos of dildos on display. This is where I discover the existence of the limp day-glo pink dildo. I buy two because there aren't any in France. (Actually there was one a few months ago, all old and dirty, at Yanko in Les Halles. I guess nobody wanted to buy it because of its colour, too surrealist.) Miles of freeway in the desert to go to the beach. We go to the gym in West Hollywood. They're like slugs cruising the Jacuzzi under the plants, like in the opening scenes of porn movies. We fuck almost nobody, just one or two guys we meet in cowboy bars in Silverlake. I fuck Quentin every day. Unheard of between us. We drink Coors in front of the TV and eat sushi I found at the supermarket down the hill. I drove very fast to get there. I'm happy.

Stéphane announced to Jean-Marc he was leaving him. Jean-Marc threw him out. I offered to let him stay at my place rather than have him look for a studio. But all the while I was telling myself I was making a mistake. I didn't have the nerve to tell him it would be better if he got his own place, I'd just started seeing him after all. I couldn't see myself doing that to him. I knew he had never lived alone and he was scared to. I told myself that if we didn't live together I would dump him, whereas if we did live together maybe I would love him as I should. I told myself I no longer knew what love was. I didn't want to be on my own. I didn't want to have to go out searching for someone any more. Stéphane would eventually acquire the qualities he was lacking, and I would love him.

7 OUR YOUTH IS FLYING BY

Saturday afternoon. We're in bed naked. The telephone rings. It's Nico. Hi what's up? I say, not too content at the idea of him turning my head around with his love problems. Not much, he says. Quentin almost killed me last night. He bashed me in the head with his boots, he kicked me all over, I've got bruises everywhere. And how do you feel now? I ask. Uh, I hurt all over, I can't walk, he answers. You want me to bring you something to eat, I say? He says Yeah, that'd be great and could you buy some yoghurt, I can't open my mouth much. OK, I'm on my way, I say. It was Nico, I tell Stéphane. Quentin almost killed him. You want to come? Sure, he says.

It's true, he's a bashed and bloody mess. I make some tea, he eats some yoghurt and bananas. Well, I say, I thought you two weren't seeing one another any more. He says In fact I did promise myself not to see him any more, after my suicide attempt ten days ago. I'd been drinking a lot you know, I said to myself You've got one hundred T4s, Quentin doesn't love you, what's the use?

I took everything there was in the medicine chest and then a friend called two hours later and I said I'm not doing so well, I took ten packs of Y and Z and I drank a bottle of scotch. He brought me to St-Louis, they pumped my stomach. And do you know what Quentin said? He said This just goes to prove what a stupid, nothing shit you are. That's when I left him. Obviously after that he tried everything to get me back. He came over Wednesday afternoon to bring back my things. He'd gone and had his hair cut, he'd even been to the tanning parlour, he'd put on his fancy shirt, the one you gave him, with orange and purple checks. As if by accident he didn't have on any underwear under his sweat pants, he said he'd forgotten to put any on, and he never stopped touching himself. Before he left I told him If you feel like fucking give me a call. Of course, the next day Hello? I feel like fucking. We saw each other Thursday night, hugs, kisses, we didn't fuck but it was great. He told me he wasn't fucking around for the time being, but on the answering machine there were nothing but messages from guys calling saying I'm calling back like we said. We saw each other again the next day. Quentin wanted to go dancing at the Queen. I wanted to fuck. He'd had an E before I got there, there weren't any left for me. He said You see chéri I dropped an E, I want to dance, I'll be back home around five and I'll really feel like fucking my brains out by then, just you stay here and relax. I stayed. At five, Quentin comes in with some dark-haired guy with ears that stick out. They have a drink in the front room, they talk rugby (the guy's a rugby player). So you'll be around next week? Can I have your number? When should I call? I caught up with him in the kitchen. I told him Quentin, enough of this, for three months you've been giving me this shit, you're fucking with me. He told me You piss me off Nico, you can see for yourself I'm not going to fuck this guy now. I slapped him in the face. He said As soon as this guy leaves you're going to pay for that. As soon as the guy left he jumped on me. Five-eleven, one hundred and ninety pounds, versus five-two, one hundred and twenty pounds. He flung me against the wall, the shelves fell on me, he beat my head and my ribs in with his boots. Stop! You're going to kill me. And then he stopped, he started weeping Mon chéri, I love you, come on let's sleep, I want us to fuck. I told him No. So he said Aha! I guess I haven't beat you up enough yet. I'll show you what a slashed-up face looks like. I love you. You won't get out of here alive. I felt like I was going to faint. I was in a rage, I kicked him in the balls with my knees, I got free, I threw him down on the bed, I got on my jacket, he got back up, he grabbed me, I smashed him in the head so I could escape. I was pissing blood everywhere. I went straight to the emergency ward.

I leave Quentin a message telling him I want to bash in his face if I ever see him, but I'm going to restrain myself. I'm too scared, in fact, he'll kill me.

The next day I meet up with Cedric in the street. I tell him things aren't going so well, Quentin almost killed his boyfriend with his Doc Martens on Friday night. We have a drink, I tell him the story. We catch up, he's very talkative, he brings the conversation back to himself pretty much. (Once, Quentin and I were over at his place and there was this picture of him on the cover of a German skin mag lying around.) He tells me he's doing better this week, they thought he had cytomegalovirus, he's got plenty of psychosomatic shit, he went for a casting to be the host of a getting-back-into-shape TV show, he just never stops fucking, he has a new boyfriend. I inquire and it turns out I know the guy. I went with Quentin to the guy's place in the country to cut wood a year ago. Quentin did him. Cedric tells me his new boyfriend loves getting fucked by him, but he hasn't fisted him yet. I ask him if this is with or without a condom. He says You know, nobody uses condoms any more, not even the Americans, everybody's positive now, I don't know any one who's negative. (Me neither, come to think of it, apart from Quentin. His last test was six months ago I believe.) And you know me, I go ahead and swallow cum. I say Yeah, that's right, cum's cool, I'd like to swallow some myself, fucking is really grand when you can do everything. He's surprised I found a new boyfriend so fast. I tell him I even had two, it's because I'm nice to them, guys get attached to me, and then when there's something about them that turns me off, I trade them in. I don't try to make a go of it. He talks to me about an editor friend of his for my diary, the one who published the book by the girl masochist, it sold ten thousand copies, she just died with her master in a car wreck, horrible. We exchange our new addresses. And then we give each other a kiss on the mouth right in front of the cops.

Two days later Stéphane and I go for a drink at the Quetzal. We run into Marc, the ex-external supporter of Peter, an ex of Quentin and mine. We chit-chat. He leaves us to say hello in the back of the bar, then returns. You and Quentin on bad terms? he asks. I'm not speaking to him any more, I say, I'm not seeing him any more, other than that, no, why? Because he's here, he says. He is indeed. Ten feet away, with Eric, our ex-housekeeper. He has on the blue bomber jacket I gave him, an old white T-shirt and blue sweat pants that are not neat. He hasn't shaved, he still has black eyes from the battle with Nico. To me he looks withered and small, wrinkled. In profile Eric says something apparently funny in his ear. I think I'm out of here this instant, I say. Off we go.

The next day I feel depressed as soon as I get up. The weather is extraordinarily beautiful. It's Saturday. I have work to do. I feel like calling him and saying Save yourself. He looked so much like an old lost baby. It's true, I say to Stéphane, I actually do want to kill him, Quentin's right about that. Maybe one of these days I'll want to kill you too. So the last thing you see before you die will be me. I love you. I kill you. And there I go all misty eyed. I get over it, with Stéphane you get over things fast. I listen to Jam and Spoon, Triptomatic Fairytales, something recommended by Christophe, another friend. The last time I saw him was in the water, the pool in Les Halles. When I asked him how he was doing he

answered Not so hot. Why not? I asked, and he said I
kicked out HIV-poz a month ago, I didn't know how
I could. Because we were in a public place I couldn't
take him in my arms. I hugged him on the sly when we
met up again at the far end of the pool.

8 POSSESSION

I enter from the front, not bad, he's a little contracted, he gives not a lot of thought to playing with my nipples although he must see I'm not that hard. I don't much feel his ass, but hey, it's not so bad, at least he isn't tight or tense. I grab him under the knees, I wedge down his arms, he can't move any more. I bang him gently, I arch my back to the max.

I fuck him exactly the way Quentin used to fuck me. First is the hold. I take him in my hands and I hold him, gently and firmly. From the front there are many possibilities. From the back there are also, but fewer. With his ankles on my shoulders, I put my arms around his neck or his hips to fuck him from the front. I hold him by the ankles, spread his legs apart: his legs are tucked in against his chest, his feet are on my abs or my sides below my ribs. If I grab him from under his knees I am able to fuck him deeper, my arms are extended and all of my weight is in my lower body. It's the best. I can also hold him by his lower back, or lift the lower part of his body slightly in the air, or by his ankles, with his legs crossed froggy-style, or else straight out and joined on my chest. I can also hold him by wrapping my arms around his thighs or his legs. These positions are the stablest, the best for mastering penetration. Moreover, by varying the angles, I can feel different parts of dick and ass each time, sometimes more the underside, sometimes more the upperside, or direct down the centre axis, a bit from above, a bit from below . . . Then there's the arch of the back. This makes you feel your dick to the maximum. The more I arch my back, the more sweeping the penetration and the better he feels it. It loosens him up for good. And then there is the shove. In the final stages of the movement, don't forget to exert stronger and stronger pressure from the pelvis to open deeper and deeper. Hold back ramming right away because later on you know you'll be able to ram for a lot longer time, and in an ass a lot moister, and you'll provoke a lot more gratitude. I fuck his ass down real deep for the first time at last and it goes on for so long before he comes that I'm able to get his real supple ass so loose that it's like slurp, slurp, slurp, and I'm covered in sweat and my thighs hurt after. Like Quentin in the past with me.

The next day I awoke before he did, around one. I puked all my dinner from the night before. I cleaned off the toilet and got back in bed. He woke up because of the noise. I asked him to fix me a bowl of hot milk and honey. As soon as I'd finished, I ran and puked it up in the toilet. It made like a wave, white and green because of the bile. I told myself I shouldn't have drunk milk. In an hour or so I drank a glass of water, which went down, and I ate two spoons of rice after. I immediately puked it all on to the tray and the bed. I fell asleep. When I awoke, I'd shit in bed. The woman doctor from SOS Médecins gave me a certificate for seven days' sick leave.

9 NO COMMENT

It's a nice day. Stéphane comes by to pick me up after
work. We go home in his car. I'm not up for doing any
fucking. This morning I told him I'd rape him when we
got home. That was to make me do it, to make his day.
But in fact it sickens me. I watch the passing scenery. I
decide to put him in a hood. This way at least I'm sure
to get hard.

I take out the one in leather because it looks more
S & M and because I'm pissed at him just now. I blindfold
him. A good idea apparently. It makes him hard. He
gives his ass gladly. I can feel he's really obsessed by his
pussy. I fuck him for an hour and a quarter. This puts
me in the mood, so the next day I decide to begin all
over again. But this time I'm not pissed at him any
more so I put him in the black latex hood. Latex is more
mysterious, more intimate I think. He comes open
slowly, millimetrically, like an apricot. I pay close attention for the first time not to hurt him in any way. I eat
the hood. I spit on it then I lick it clean with big swipes
of the tongue, banging him at the same time. He moans

softly. He hangs from my tits. He's the way I was when I discovered my ass with Quentin five years ago. I fuck him for an hour and a half.

I fuck him until I realise that once again I won't feel like coming. At this moment I'd rather be dead. I go faster to get it over with. When he comes I pull out of his ass and I remove my condom and I think of squirting on the hole and smearing to make the death penetrate nicely and I jerk off and then my ultra-swollen dick once again takes over and since I'm close to coming I'm not thinking any more and I explode in a geyser and it's like in a super-fine porn movie and right after that I start thinking again.

10 ATTEMPT

It's a nice day. I go and have my breakfast on the terrace of the Bon Pêcheur. Ten a.m. The neighbourhood is still empty at this hour. Very calm. I go back home, running a few errands along the way. I call Stéphane at work. He takes the call. He says Hello I'm in a meeting now, can I call you back? I say No, no need, I'm calling just to let you know that when you come home this evening I'll have a dildo up my ass and a hood on, and handcuffs so all you'll have to do is fasten them up and then savage me. He says OK, that's perfect, very businesslike. I say What time do you think you'll get here? He says Eight o'clock.

At eight-ten he buzzes. I open the door. He looks real turned on. I do a U-turn. I cross my wrists to let him fasten the handcuffs to the big leash hanging off my back. Click. I start getting hard. He enters, closes the door behind him. I'm already on my knees in front of his crotch. I open my mouth to the max, it's difficult because of the leather hood, he zips down his fly as fast as he can, takes out his half-hard dick. I take advantage of this and swallow it down whole, to the pubes. I go at it good. He gets big fast. This makes my mouth gag, but then I come back down and I take it in, all of it, the head goes behind my glottis. Like this I wag him with the back of my throat, I breathe as I can, through my nose, drooling and slobbering.

Five good minutes I've been sucking, I'm coming down. I start sucking less enthusiastically, I do the cock longways, I suck only the head. Not for long, since he grabs me by the top of the hood and forces me all the way back down. This turns me on again big time. A moment later he pulls backwards on my head. He looks down on me. Little slut! He spits on me. Whoa! I'm so glad it's starting back up so good I do a thing I don't do usually because I think it's dirty but right now I want to show just who is who tonight. I drop down and begin licking his boots. At the same time, I spread my knees and I rear my shoulders all the way back to present my ass in style. I know it's a friendly enough sight: hairy at the centre except for the crack, which is shaved clean, and emerging from my hole, the balls and the pink day-glo end of the dildo, held in place only by the thong of my leather jock strap. Higher up, he can see my hands, fastened to the leash that's hanging from the middle of my back, and higher still the leather dog collar around my neck and the hood, laced up at the back. To get a more vulnerable look I didn't put my chaps on, but I do have on my Rangers, and thick brown synthetic socks, a little trashy, rolled down over them.

He smacks my ass. When this gets to be too much, I

come back up and suck on his balls and cock. He stops me, pushes me down to the floor, he's a bit rough but that's too bad, this is no time to make any remarks, he grabs me by the neck, he pulls me toward the bedroom. I make my way the best I can, half on my knees, half crawling. He takes advantage of this and smacks my ass real hard. On arrival at the bedroom he takes me by the shoulders, throws me on the bed, I get into position, my chest on the foot of the bed, I'm still down on my knees, my ass up in the air, no, it's not what he wants, he makes me move up on the bed, I get back into position, my Rangers spread real wide in the void, I lower my ass so that it's not too high for his dick, he goes for a condom, he puts one on, he smacks my ass two, three times, he pulls the thong aside, the dildo begins coming out on its own, he pushes it all the way back in, once, twice, and then he plucks it out, he throws it on the bed, he puts his big dick in for a change and he fucks me like a queen.

We never do it this way again. I think it would be pointless to make him do an exact repeat, so I wait for him to propose something. He doesn't.

11 BACK FROM HOLIDAY

I pick up the mail. Quentin has written me. I read Part One of our story is over. Part Two not yet begun. I'm sorry I made you suffer. I long to hear you, to talk to you calmly, in a garden. I show Stéphane the letter. Stéphane says It could be from Jean-Marc. I think I don't think so.

I'm in a rage. I put away our things, I load the washing machine, I throw out stuff that's gone rotten in the fridge, I'm not hungry. I have a hard time falling asleep in spite of the two beers at the QG and the joint. The neighbour's guests leave at three in the morning. Car doors slam, the diesel warms up. The front door trembles, creaks, screeches. I jump to the window. I'd like to mow them down with a machine gun like in *Taxi Driver*. I rehearse the phone call I'm going to make to the building manager. First version, second version, third version.

The next day I don't go in to work. Stéphane finally comes home. I order him down on all fours to suck me while I finish rolling a joint. I spread my legs real wide to look at my dick. I'm stripped down to nothing but my hi-tops and soccer socks hiked up. I tell him to put a butt-plug up his ass and put on nipple clamps. I hand-cuff him. Leather handcuffs, one for each wrist. They're more bracelets than handcuffs, they don't hurt, you can wear them for hours. Then I put him in the black leather dog collar. I fasten each handcuff to rings that are on each side of the collar for that purpose. I bind the handcuffs to the top of each thigh with rope, then to the nipple clamps. Now the slightest movement from him and he'll get strangled a little, pinched a little, just enough for it to be like two hands squeezing, but not enough really to hurt. Pain is not the aim of the game.

I fuck him from behind, gently whipping him with the riding crop. I say Give me an ass wide open now. He gives me an ass wide open. And then I say Now close it. He closes it. It's real nice. From the back, his hands cuffed behind his neck, his hard-on's been raging a good quarter of an hour without him touching it. I undo one of his hands so he can pull on my balls. He's forbidden to pull on himself of course. I tie him back up.

I push him on to the bed to fuck him lying flat. And then I begin to get real bored. So I put a pillow over his head. I push down. This turns me on. Him too by the way. His ass perks up a full tilt. I push down harder. An orgasm starts rising. I push down harder and harder and then I have to stop because it's getting risky. The orgasm stops rising and I know there's nothing more to do to bring it back, so I change his position and I ram him to make him come and he comes and I come out and jerk off and I lie down next to him after without touching him. I close my eyes. In a while he asks me what's wrong. I say I'd like to bump off the whole wide world, smash all my toys, stay all alone in the blood and scream till I die. He says that would make a nice scene in a movie.

12 CONSULTATION

I explain to my doctor that my T4s have gone back up. They were down the last time I saw her, but I was over-exhausted, I'd just moved, I'd left the man I'd been with for five years, he was threatening to throw acid on my face. The problem is, I say to her, I'm bored with the new one, he doesn't thrill me, the other one was crazy and I loved him, it's always the less crazy of the two who's crazy about the crazier one, and the crazier one is only crazy about himself it seems. There's no way around it, she tells me. That's the way it is. Either you're reasonable and you see somebody normal and you're bored, or you see somebody crazy who wants to throw acid on your face and you have a good time. That's the way it is. I tell her I was depressed about it for four years, but now that I've matured maybe things could work out with Quentin. I read this weekend in a magazine that what works with pathological seducers is somebody who's extremely reassuring and who knows the way to enter their game, with a touch of perversity if possible. She asks me Where is he now, has he gone away? He's three blocks from me, I tell her.

She gives me her usual concerned check-up. My doctor has real round blue eyes, a round, very rimmed mouth, a round head, brown hair. She's young and she knows her shit. And your work, she asks? I talk to her about my book. And what's the subject? I laugh and tell her it's the same as Moderne Mesclun's in *Agrippine*. Have you read *Agrippine*? She's in a café with her uncle and he's talking to her about his projects, among others, his erotic autobiography set to a background of Gregorian rap. I tell her that my book is erotic autobiography, set to a background of Gregorian rap, because when I write I listen to Depeche Mode.

I tell her Quentin wrote me. I tell her I replied to his letter on the back of the final electricity cut off notice I received because his electricity is still in my name. I wrote I don't know how to answer just now. Guillaume. My doctor observes, with finesse, that this does not mean no.

13 COMPULSION

I go to Marks & Spencer by the Opéra. I first explore
Foods entirely, then I go upstairs to Menswear, where
I examine the underwear, and afterwards the sales. I
curb an impulse to buy things that aren't useful or
portable. I buy, all the same, two pairs of tight-fitting
blue thermal long johns for winter and then four pairs
of barely black socks, ten francs a pair, primarily cotton,
two with designs, two without designs, and then I find
a great dark grey wool winter sports jacket marked way
down, for Stéphane. Then I go back downstairs to Foods
and I buy some coleslaw and some inexpensive white
Australian wine that looks good, some fresh spinach in
a microwave oven bag, some fresh mini cocktail sausages
ready to grill (two rows six different sorts), and a round
triple tray with carrot and nut salad, bean salad and
coleslaw, and then some matured orange Cheddar and
some whole-wheat muffins, some stir-fry vegetables (soy
beans, carrots, mushrooms) and some smoked Canadian
bacon. Some baked beans in tomato sauce. I get the real

recipe, not the Boston spicy, but the basic English one you eat in the morning with eggs and toast.

Marks & Spencer is fascinating. There's nothing left for one to do. Everything's been prepared, the egg-and-watercress sandwiches, the chicken tikka meatballs, the Irish salmon brochettes, the shrimp cocktail, the cole-slaw, the vegetables washed and cut and ready to fry, the pork pies, the square cheeses. The one blight in the store are the gâteaux. Even the cakes look average. A question of generation. The store's buyers are surely more into bean sprouts and cherry tomato salad than mince pie and pudding. I go home like a jerk on the métro with my tons of shopping bags. Soon there'll be a Marks & Spencer at Hôtel de Ville. That will be nice.

Once I'm back home I put away the fresh foods in the fridge and then I put on a pair of the long johns and I smoke a joint and I jerk off and then I sleep. I wake up when Stéphane turns his key in the door. I send him to the front room to try on his new jacket before he gets his clothes off. The jacket looks good on him, I knew it would, it's the same cut as the blue and the green ones that go so well on him. He won't be able to say I don't look after him.

14 LIVING IN THE GHETTO

Sunday night at the Loco I ran into Tom. He told me his ex was dead. Only on the way home did I think about inviting him to dinner the evening after with two of Stéphane's friends. I left a message on his machine when I got in from shopping. He called back to say he would come.

At dinner Stéphane found out a guy he knew from Act-up is dead. It flipped him out but he didn't speak to me about it until the next day. The guests went home. I was horny. We'd drunk five bottles for five of us. I said to Stéphane I want to fuck you in a sling in a fuck bar. He washed his ass before we left. I took along condoms and xylocaine. I was already depressed. We got there. I fucked him in a sling in a stall. The chains had two hoops too many that went clink clink clink, the sling was a little too high, I had to get on my tiptoes to get in with any depth. My hard-on was soft, then harder, then softer, then harder. It went on like this a good half-hour. I said All right, let's finish up at home, it's more comfortable. I didn't say a word in the car. We went

back upstairs. I rolled a joint in silence. We began again.
I was losing my hard-on. I wound up saying loads of
horrible things to him. You're not a turn-on, there are
no surprises with you, you don't know how to play with
my nipples, I'm bored to shit in your ass, excuse me but
right now I'm depressed, I'd rather you fuck me. Or else
I fuck you without a condom. He said Fuck me without
a condom. Instantly my hard-on sprang back. I thought
In any case I don't have pre-cum and I can surely avoid
squirting in his ass. I went back in. Five minutes later
of course I was ready to come, whereas, with a condom
on I usually never do, I'm at such a distance. I said I'm
ready to come. He said Go ahead. I said I think we'd
better wait for the results of your test. He'd never been
tested. He's persuaded himself he has HIV anyway. I'd
pushed him to have the test done. I say We'll do this
later. I come out and shoot all over his hungry bitch
little ass.

The week after, the test is negative. I tell myself I did
the right thing not coming in his ass. And then I feel
alone. Disappointed. And then alone.

15 PEOPLE ARE STILL HAVING SEX

I live in a wonderful world where the whole world has
been to bed with the whole world. The map to this
world is found in the community magazines I read
assiduously. Bars. Clubs. Restaurants. Saunas. Minitel.
Party lines. Cruising spots. And all the telephone
numbers and addresses and first names that go with
them. In this world every man has fucked at least five
hundred other men, in large part the same ones for that
matter. The men who go out. But the networks do not
criss-cross exactly. There are the men more into bars.
More into clubs. More into bars and clubs. More into
saunas. More into party lines. More into Minitel. More
into dark hair. More into blond. More into muscles.
More into rough sex. More into the classic fuck. Take
your pick. You've got a lot to pick from. And nobody's
looking to start a family. You are one or no more than
two in this world except when there's a slave at home
for a more or less long time. I think it's fine all this
inventiveness. I have a friend who put his two hands
around his boyfriend's hand inside the ass of some guy

who's well known in the community, who also has his tits and cock pierced, and is fitted out with an impressive array of equipment he shares generously with quite a lot of people.

Like I do with what I've got at home in a little closet in the bedroom, on five levels. On the very top there's the cumbersome stuff: two pairs of chaps, one in leather, one in latex, a douche bag and its tube, plus an enormous cone-shaped dildo for sitting down on. Under that there are dildos and butt-plugs arranged by size on two shelves: two fat butt-plugs and four small ones, four two-headed dildos, eight ordinary dildos. Under that, the little material hanging on nails: five different pairs of nipple clamps, some clothespins, a parachute for the balls, a dog collar, two hoods, one in leather, one in latex, six cockrings, in steel or leather, regular or with built-in ball squeezers, two dick sheaths (a regular one in adjustable leather and one with spike tips pointing in, a little outrageous this one), a riding crop, a small whip, a black bandanna and a red bandanna for gagging or tying up, a channelled tube gag that directs piss right into the throat, a ball gag, the ball is inflatable, nipple clamps mounted on an extendible leather Y that can be linked to a cockring so the crotch can pull the nipples, a leaded ball-stretcher, not too heavy, three-hundred grams and, at three centimetres, not so wide either and placed between the cock and the balls or else like a normal cockring, two pairs of leather handcuffs, a leather collar with handcuffs that may be worn around the back or the front, depending on which side it's placed. At the very bottom, there's cumbersome stuff again: an adjust-able iron bar with leather-tipped handcuffs, a leather harness, two pairs of Rangers, my stormtrooper boots.

I've been buying these things for years. A lot of them. I've chucked out plenty of junk I'd bought without a clue, dildos too rigid or too crooked, cockrings too tight, clamps too strong. I've kept only this. The bare essential. I have within arm's reach everything I need. Alcohol. Hash. Acid. Es. Coke. Weed. Poppers. Sex mags. Sex cassettes. A Polaroid.

Certain elements are more useful than others. I love them all. They are like parts of me. They stay where I decide, maintaining my hold over them. But it is also their duty to serve the body. Hood collar gag nipple clamps handcuffs dildos cockring cock-choker para-chute handcuffs. Head mouth neck tits wrists arms ass crotch cock balls ankles legs. All are put to work. Ready to maximise the effects of the dick in the mouth or in the ass, the strokes of the crop on the ass, the legs the back the shoulders the arms the hands the feet the balls the cock. It never hurts when it's done right. I'm no sadist. Only a little megalomaniac. This leaves no marks. In any case, whatever I do, whatever I use has been tried out on me beforehand. So everything goes off without a hitch. Even the big dildos come out without a trickle of blood, even the ones that are fatter than a fist and that make it past the second sphincter. I've become very conscious of my body, of its exterior, of its interior, thanks to all his, I think. I train. My nipples, my ass. I practise. My ejaculations, my performance.

I wonder if it's sinister or if it's right. I think about what Jeanne Moreau says to her niece in an American movie where she's old and extravagant. No, she tells her. I don't think you're stupid. I think you've lost hope. You should do nothing. Absolutely nothing. Until hope returns. Like she's sure it always returns. Maybe she's right. I tried last night. Instead of cruising the Minitel or going out for a drink in a bar as I usually would, I waited. In a few minutes hope really did return. It returned by my left leg, I felt it. A muscular appeasement. All the queers I know work out. If not, they swim. They are, almost all of them, HIV-positive. It's crazy how they last. They still go out. They still fuck. Plenty of them get crap like meningitis, diarrhoea, a case of shingles or Kaposi or pneumocystosis. And then they're all right. Just a little skinnier, some of them. The ones that get a CMV or other more freaky crap haven't been seen around in general for some time already. They aren't talked about. This said, none of my close buddies has died. Four guys I fucked are dead that I know of. I suspect others. Not a lot. People don't die a lot apparently. They say AIDS is evolving towards a thing like diabetes. That as long as Social Security has the coins we'll be treated for whatever crops up.

It's been a few years now since I entered this world. I spend most of my time there. I prefer to go to London on vacation too rather than discover Budapest. Budapest, that'll be for later. We're doing fine in the ghetto. There's a lot of people. More people all the time. Queers who start fucking all the time and no longer go as often as before into the normal world. Apart from the job, in general, and seeing the family, everything can be done without going out of the ghetto. Sports, shopping, movies, eating out, vacations. There aren't ghettos everywhere. There's the centre of Paris. There's London, Amsterdam, Berlin, New York, San Francisco, Los Angeles, Sydney. In the summer there's Ibiza, Sitges, Fire Island, Mykonos, Majorca. Sex is the centrepiece. Everything turns around it: the clothes, the short hair, the nice body, the sex toys, the junk you take, the alcohol you drink, the junk you read, the junk you eat, mustn't be too heavy when you go out or you might not get to fuck. You rarely go home alone if you persist until late and you're not too depressed, if you don't tell yourself you've already had all the guys in the place worth having. Or all the ones you know you can get. But often you are able to get the ones you thought you couldn't. You progress.

Last night Stéphane was recuperating from the weekend. I couldn't sleep as usual when I'm not over-exhausted. I wondered if I would live alone or move back in with him in three months. I gave my notice. I couldn't stand the apartment anymore. There's this project to have a terrace I could never pay for if I live alone. I began sorting out my sex mags, tearing out pages I thought were a turn-on. I made a tableau on the living-room floor with them. Six square meters of pictures of dicks, a few asses too, but cocks especially, hard for the most part, quite pretty. It wasn't bad. When I got through I sat down on the sofa and I jerked off looking at them, drinking a Heineken and sniffing poppers. After, around three, I got into bed. I live in a world where plenty of things I thought impossible are possible.

PART TWO

1 SERGE THE BEAUTY

We met him at the Queen fairly late, at an hour when
there's practically nobody left but fanatic clubbers.
Going bald. Six-one, one hundred and seventy-five
pounds. Body a knockout. White even-spaced teeth in
perpetual smile. Sufficiently young. Nice face. Visibly
blitzed on some high-quality stuff. First we looked at
each other. Then I was dancing, clinging to Stéphane,
to turn him on. He moved in. We were putting on a
show on the dance floor, making like we were humping
one another. This got a rise out of him. I felt quantity
there. Then we got unglued and we exchanged a few
words through the din of the music. I sent Stéphane to
get us something to drink. To the other one I said Man
do I ever want to blow you. He said No problem. He
led me off to the toilets. I said to myself Cool, he knows
what he wants. I followed with no resistance. There was
a traffic jam at the toilets, a whole line to get in. I said
All right what do we do? He dragged me over to a blind
spot just by the doorway.

He turned his back to the dance floor. I let myself

slide to my knees. He brought out his mega-beautiful dick and I took it in my face and jerked off five minutes or so. This was hot. Then I said Look my boyfriend is waiting for us, we gotta go over to him, OK? He said OK. Stéphane was waiting at the bar with the drinks, very cool as always.

We rather rapidly agreed as to the next steps. First, we stop by his place to do a new American drug I haven't heard of that's supposed to be great for fucking, and after we go home because we have toys at our place and he doesn't at his. By now I'm fairly convinced that this is going to be more trouble than it's worth because of this final detail, but he is such a specimen I cannot imagine one single second not getting him when I can.

His apartment is tiptop. Loft space. TV and speakers in the bathroom. Classy furniture. An envelope addressed to him from a TV network is lying on the extra-large counter of his eat-in American kitchen. He puts on Trance very loud. The sound is the best. We taste his powder. In ten minutes we are wiped out. Lights camera action. Our clothes peel off. He is sublime. Great dick, very large and long, big balls with lots of skin. I suck him. I lick his balls. He smacks my back, my ass. He plays macho man. I like. He's like, You're a real slut, a true one. You get me all hot and bothered. I check. He exaggerates. I'm sure he's not going to bang me but too bad. In the bathroom there was an old box of Prophyltex, full, and Prophyltex is much too tight for a cock like his. If he was using condoms inside an ass with any frequency he'd have Manix large. What's weird also is a pair of very classy women's high heels on the floor by the mirror in his bedroom. But it's the only trace of woman in the whole space. Maybe he's bi, the pretentious prick. He looks me in the eye. I do the same. We smile. He tells me Don't you look at me like that if you don't want me marrying you. I tell him It's not my fault, that's the way it is. He's like, wow wow wow!, clapping his hands while I paddle his ass with my hands to make for a sexier ambience. And then the darling is too stoned, and falls asleep on the parquet with his leather pants down to his ankles. I like this Serge, that's for sure, it's like being in love. The problem is, of course, he's not fucking me. Just a bump or two of the cock, no condom, like that, in the kitchen, the windows open, after he's snapped his cordless telephone antenna trying to insert it up my ass. This guy is not used to fucking, it shows. True you can't have everything in life. He tells me several times how sorry he is he's so wasted. I tell him no big deal.

He falls asleep on the sofa while I'm sucking him. The stereo plays opera now, this must be what he usually listens to. I'm left alone. I go into his bedroom, I scope out a few books, a method for a perfect body and how to train it, under the table by the bed, the cassettes under the TV in front of the bed, no porn or else they're well hidden, a dresser with jockey shorts, boxer shorts, socks, pocket squares. Everything is perfect. The jockey shorts are perfect. I try on a pair of blue jockey shorts, not bad, then a jockstrap, not nice (I used to have the same one almost), then an old pair of Nikos, ultra-hot cut that look great on me. I put them in my jacket, then I search for a container for the powder. I find an empty film container on his desk. I extract my little present. I wolf down a slice of all-bran bread. There's nothing else in the fridge. The opera's still on. I wake Stéphane. You all right? He's OK. I leave Serge the beauty a note with our telephone number. It's nice outside. I put on dark glasses. The streets are already coming to life. We go home. Stéphane drives. Parking lot. Pains au chocolat. Croissants. The baker's son is still our fan. It's good to be home. So we smoke a joint. And I fuck Stéphane.

He calls around seven, eight in the evening. Hi, it's Sergio. That's what I called him in my note. He's going to dinner, but we can meet up later. He is weird. He says I'll call back at midnight. All right, this is normal, with three it's always a little complicated. But for once there's someone who interests me. Makes an impression the Fuck. I'm sure he's not even going to call me back.

He calls back, only it's one-thirty. This looks bad. He apologises. I cut him short. His dinner's not over, can we meet at the Folies at three, no better make it three-thirty? I say OK. I hang up. I tell Stéphane Look, I want this fuck so bad just this once for real. I've got to go. Stéphane says it's not a problem.

2 RENDEZVOUS

I'm at the Folies Pigalle. There's a very beautiful girl in a hot pink ultra form-fitting T-shirt, with Babie written in silver. She dances great. She's as flashy as a faggot or a black. It's three o'clock. I did a quarter hit of acid, three lines of coke, smoked two joints and drank a beer at home before going out. High, but not too high. I chat with a cab driver. On the door of the Folies there's a guy Quentin and I had a three-way with ages ago. He says hi to me. Are you with somebody? A wave of paranoia, I don't understand what he wants to say, I tell him no I'm by myself, can I come in? He looks at me a little surprised but he's got to see I'm stoned. Once I'm in I tell myself obviously he's not going to turn away somebody he knows. And I think Wow, it's cool, I know the doorman at the Folies. This sort of stuff impresses me. I know it's stupid. Then there's a Chinese guy at the entrance, one of the organisers, he's real real tall and thin, he makes come-fuck-me T-shirts as a sideline. I ran into him at a fashion show my friend Georges took me to. He bends over nearly in two and gives me this lifeless kiss. Hi! I buy myself a beer. I smoke. I dance.

Tonight I know absolutely not a soul in here. No buddy, no pick-up, nobody I've ever exchanged more than two words with before. This stresses me a little. Plus, the acid's strong. It gives me these pains in the back and it pulls on the cheekbones and I'm speeding, zooming, and from time to time I'm a little short of breath and I have hot rushes. I calm down, tell myself it's always like this on acid. There are the positive sides too, the light and the colours are ten times more real than in reality. Since I'm having a good trip I can't think about anything disagreeable for more than two seconds. My one and only preoccupation has to do with what I'm feeling and this absolute necessity of mine to move, to discharge the really excessive energy the acid gives me.

Only three o'clock. I decided to be here at two-thirty to be sure not to miss him. I get off on playing the ditz. The music is good, the sound is better than before and makes me dance. When I take acid dancing relaxes my back. First I warm up, and then when I'm really cooking I get up on the stage, I take off my T-shirt, I dance with no shirt, my suspenders trailing down my thighs on top of my combat boots. It's best to have on big shoes when you have a tendency to fall around.

And then the music turns not as good, too hardcore. I come off the stage. I'm dripping sweat. I go to the toilet to freshen up. Long pink corridor. There are some North African girls getting a rise out of some North

African guys. One of the girl's saying she can piss like a guy, in the urinal. I wasn't able to piss anyhow, so I move away for her to show us. She comes up, unzips, and then she chickens out. They jabber a little aggressively, that's North Africa cruising. I go to empty my bladder in a closed stall that opens just then. The ambience is bizarre tonight.

The evening is a mega-success I think. There are only beautiful people who dance so well everybody looks filled with wonder, totally trashed or else very new to the club scene, or even both. Nothing to cruise. Too trendy. Whatever. Acid makes it OK.

I don't care so much for acid, I think it's too strong, but all right, let's face it, acid does give you zip. As soon as the music is a little less hardcore Trance, I go back and dance all the way down. Hard-hitting DJ chains together deep disco shake-that-ass, Trance pumped up to where it is almost too much really, the dance floor begins to lay down its arms when UP! it begins all over again. Guys cry out in pain when the DJ breaks the rhythm on purpose in the middle of a mix. I take a break. Stairways. Gallery. Bar. I'm covered in sweat, looking a little too hardcore for a place like this, I'm not served right away, but in the end it's OK, the gin and peppermint is good.

Ten to four and he's a no-show. I go out alone. I walk around the Place Pigalle. I'm in a rage. When I get to the Transfert the doorman smiles at me. Stéphane is there, with his big gentle eyes, a slutty tank top plunging to his tits. A kiss of the tongue and then I say What's up, cutie? He says Nothing, I was getting a little bored. The fucking fuck bar. The anniversary of the Transfert. Nothing is worse than a festive occasion in an S & M venue. Cake is being passed around on paper plates. Nobody wants any, but to be polite the guys closest to the bar force themselves. The bartender has his little tantrum: No cake gentlemen? Well let me remind you there are plenty of people out there who would.

I go around the back of the backroom, suck a little the skinhead boy hanging out naked in the big sink everybody uses for pissing. What he wants in fact is my piss, but I don't want to piss. I split. I get a few kisses, two guys tweak my nipples. I do the same to them. The guy in front of me sticks two fingers up my ass. I pull up my pants. I turn around. There's a guy in front of me I know but haven't got around to yet. He goes out all the time but I don't think he does a lot of fucking. He looks at my cock. I stroke it a little in front of him for fun. I have a discussion with a little skinhead who looks like a mouse. He's extra sweet. I tell him You make me want to do bad things. He's like, I do?, full of hope. But I'm not that convinced, I don't think he's slutty enough. He senses this as well, and we let things go at that. I go back to Stéphane at the bar. We get champagne squirted all over our face. This is beginning to weigh down on me. We decide to leave.

In the car I'm wiped. Stéphane tells me five or six times he wants sex. I don't answer. When we peel off our clothing at home, the carpet around the bed gets covered with confetti. I say to Stéphane If you want to get fucked I can do it. He doesn't look like he believes. I ask Is your ass clean? He says Yes. I take out an Olla, we don't have any Manix large, but I really like Olla. They're the ones we used in the Quentin days. They are kind of thick, but very supple and soft. I bang him first standing in front of the toilet. I make him put his head in and I fuck him. Then I bring him back to the bedroom and I fuck him on the bed, from the front, then from behind. It lasts a long time, and it's really not bad, I enter and I exit, his ass is like slurp, slurp slurp, very loud, he groans and moans, bunched up under me. I begin to lose my hard-on, his ass is too wide. I continue though. And then we have to stop because I've gone too soft. We go wash our hands. I propose he fuck me. He says he wants to piss. I flop into the tub and he pisses on me and I don't wash it off and we return to the bed. The fucking is great. Deep. Long. I let myself get fucked like never before. I find he's getting better and better. And then it becomes obvious we're too stoned to come. I search around for my watch. It's ten o'clock, we've been fucking four hours. We finish off the easy way, he licks my balls, I come, and then I offer to work over his ass with my left hand because my right hand's got cum all over it. He explodes. We cuddle. I roll one last joint. He falls asleep. I smoke half and then I realise I'm losing consciousness so I put the joint down and fall asleep.

I awake livid because of the no-show last night. We watch TV. I try to resist and then give in and call Serge around seven in the evening. Machine. I speak in case he's screening. He picks up.

—Yes?

—Hi, it's Guillaume.

—Hi, you all right?

—No.

—Ahh . . . I have people over right now, my mom.

—That's nice.

—How was it last night?

I think this over.

—It was disappointing. I mean I didn't know you weren't going to come.

—Me neither. I didn't know I wasn't going to come.

Silence.

—Well, I go on, you're with people and anyway I don't have a whole lot else to tell you. It's up to you.

—I'll call you back.

—OK.

I hang up. This guy makes me sick. Do you realise he stands me up and I call him back, I say to Stéphane? But this is what's good about it too. Being impressed. Showing it. Like a slut. But not too much. I was happy that it had been disappointing. I was hoping he'd understand I meant to say both that he was a disappointment and that I was disappointed. I wanted to rattle his cage a little. But at the same time I still wanted him. His ultra-soft skin. His perfect muscles, not too big, not too small. Beautiful.

3 EXCESS

This weekend the cousin of my friend M died. She had third-degree burns from an accident last year. Jojo, the man who helped out my mother with the gardening, shot himself in the head. Terrier is on a rest cure in the country following a suicide attempt. All is well.

Thursday night I went out on my own again. Stéphane was sleeping. He was frazzled from the job and the rhythm I impose on him combined. I was totally awake and in great shape of course. I'd got up at one in the afternoon. I didn't take anything before I went out. I went to the QG. Nobody there. Then to a groove party near here, semi-deserted. After that it was time to go to the Queen. Men's night. Let's just say a few more men than usual. I know the faces. I dance. I schmooze. An older fellow, a tall black American, around forty-five, tells me he has coke he brought back from the States. I tell myself this just might be the real thing. I ask if I can taste it. He says for that we have to go to his place. I end up in a taxi going to the Avenue de la Grande Armée.

Four other younger and cuter blacks are playing cards in the front room. He steers me straight into his room so I won't hit on any of them, the old veteran. OK. We do way too much coke on a corner of his business card. Normally coke makes you jumpy, but when you do a whole lot, more than half a gram, say, in a short period, it rather drags you down, a bit like heroin, but not as solemn. I don't give a fuck though. I came here for this, and plus the old timer is getting more and more wasted, and that's fine with me because I don't really want to fuck anyway, not him. I roll a joint from the lump of hash I brought with me just in case. We smoke. We drink a beer. We do more coke. I want some head and I want some tail, he says. I suck his big black half-hard dick a long time. He's mega-wrecked and so am I. Finally, it's cool fucking this way, too fucked up. He sucks me too for a good while. I let myself go. I suck him some more. I ask again for coke. We do more coke. He rims me. And then he says he wants to fuck me. This is without a condom of course, judging from the ambience and the droop of his erection. I tell myself that even with no condom it's not very risky, at any rate he'll never be able to come. Are you positive? I ask, legs in the air. Yeah, the Baloo bear answers me. He has one fuck of a time getting his dick in, but eventually he does. He fucks me for a little while though. I think he must have been a very good fuck before. We stop because he's getting too limp. I ask him for a beer. While he's gone I put in my pocket a worn jockstrap by Gazelle, New York, lying on the floor.

I came home at six, after I'd stopped by the Transfert where nobody was left. I began in the bathroom with the dildos, sitting on the maxi butt-plug I have that's twelve inches high and twelve around the base. I knew only too well I wouldn't be able to take the whole thing, actually I only know one guy who can, it was just that I was lazy and it's the only big toy in my collection that stands up by itself. The job it did was just average because after a while the coccyx starts to hurt. Even so, I was still making a lot of noise with my ass. I heard Stéphane moving around in the next room. I said You sleeping? He answered No. I kept wanking. He came into the bathroom. He looked shattered when he saw what I was doing. I said You OK? He nodded. I said Well then would you mind shoving this in me? I'm getting nowhere by myself. He said No. I said All right then let's go. I snatched up a towel, chose the utensils. I didn't roll a joint, I didn't want to over-indulge. Fucked-up as I was, with a good hit of poppers I knew it would go in, so I selected the replica of Kris Lord's dick (10x7) and then the enormous double-header from San Francisco, bigger than an arm. It was great. First of all, he fucked me good with the Lord. Then I asked for a change. Not only did the monster go in with no trouble, but I was able to get my chimney swept a good ten minutes. I said I was going to come. He pulled it out. I came all over myself, in convulsive jolts. Since it was seven, Stéphane went to work. I slept.

4 A LITTLE SWEETNESS

On Friday I went to work with M who had her little three-month-old cousin at her place, the son of the deceased. I took him in my arms. I noticed, when he started gaining confidence, that he looked at me the way Stéphane looks at me. I liked it. Then I walked home along the quays. Then I fucked Stéphane. It was the first time I fucked him again after a week of abstinence. I had a big hard-on. I put a finger in him then two and then I went in on the first pop with the head of my dick past the second sphincter. Like with Terrier, but better because I've made some progress these nine months. It was the best.

Then we went out to dinner and then out to the Queen. We got there around three, a little early for entering without waiting in line, but I have an in with Sandrine at the door. So I roll up very cool, not a doubt in my mind, but still they put you through all these changes at the door, too many people, guys getting thrown out, the bouncers stop me. Who said you could come in, sir? Stand back. All right, I don't care, I know

I'm in. And Sandrine is like OK, the OK that means we grease past the suburbans without paying, then on down the stairs. It's ultra-jammed, there're lines at the bar, lines for the urinals, packed, the music is excellent, I almost always want to dance. I'm just a little surprised to be doing what I'm doing not high.

Sunday night. Terrier tells me on the phone that his pharmacist now renews his Xanax without a prescription. And also he had a real hot Iranian who lives right near me and who, in this order, fisted him (the first time in his life), put a dildo in him, fucked him. The guy fucking pissed on him for the finale. I say to him I consider it your duty to give me his telephone number. He tells me that he didn't take it. I tell him that's just like him. He tells me No, it's like this. At seven in the morning we were buzzed on beer and hash, the guy told me I could sleep there, I preferred going home. And you didn't ask for his number, I ask? He says No I didn't ask for his number because he had slipped it to me without my asking, but I tossed it on my way home. Say it isn't so, I say. It is, he says. You are really screwy, I say. No I'm not, he says, I threw it out because I didn't like him that much, that's all. We debate, for the sake of principle, whether he should have given me the number if he'd had it.

Terrier's in good shape these days. He's cut out the Prozac and some other thing so he now just takes Xanax because if he doesn't he has the shakes. He goes out every night. I tell him I think it takes courage to slip out alone into the night, to go do who knows what with who knows whom. He tells me he has to go to Dieppe soon to see a fuck buddy who's forty and has a château. Today the guy asked him to get information on the Caribbean, two weeks in October. The guy hasn't poked him yet, just the dildo. It was nice, so he says. The guy has all the right toys: clamps, dildos, latex chaps, leather briefs. Terrier says Yeah but for me he's too femme and I don't like that, I need a more solid man.

We talk a while longer and then I tell myself Stéphane's maybe a little tired of hearing me having such fun with his predecessor so I cut it short. Terrier and I are getting along these days. He's now got used to the idea we won't live together ever again. He doesn't douse my doormat with turpentine any more, he doesn't slice his face with the razor blade any more (actually he'd done this with such care the gashes went away completely in five days). Anyway, it's going all right. We'll be able to resume the guided tours of Paris we take by day. I prefer not bringing him along to pick out fuck movies at the sex shop any more, for reasons I should have been able to see from the start. In fact I knew this wasn't a good thing to do. But it turned me on to torture him some.

I come close to Stéphane in bed. He snuggles up in my arms. You are like a croissant, I say to him. Butter or ordinary? he says. Butter, I tell him. But I'm also a little ordinary, he says. That's true, I say, but you're intelligent. So it goes by.

It's midnight. Stéphane is sleeping. Tomorrow is Monday and as usual he has to get up early. I look at

him. I think he looks extra fucking hot tonight. He didn't
get a lot of sleep last night. After the Queen we went
by the Transfert and brought home some very handsome
hunk, brown hair, extra-large dick, which means we
went to bed at eight a.m. Stéphane got up at eleven to
go have lunch with a friend. Since he hadn't seen her
in a year he didn't want to put her off. He came home
around five. He told me that she had found him changed,
for the better. That she asked him how things were
going with me. That he told her He brings me to the
edge of the deep, and then we set off on a hang-glider.
He says that H told him I must be some guy. I had a
shiver. I didn't say anything.

I toss and turn unable to sleep thinking about Serge.
As though he had taken the place of Quentin. I have a
notion to call him back. Tell him I want your head. I
want your skin. I want to do something to him. I want
him to tell me to come over. I would sit enthroned on
his bed with the remote control in front of the big TV.
We would search ourselves. The demons.

5 PROBLEMS

Stéphane comes back from his friend the eye doctor. The black stars he's been having in front of his eyes for the last two weeks are a detached retina. He might lose an eye. They have to operate immediately. It figures, I think, he doesn't want to see what is happening with me. He's going into hospital the day after. He comes by after work to pick up some things. I'm in bed, out of it. You want me to go with you, I say? No no, he says, it's not worth the trouble. And so I don't go with him. I make myself something to eat. And then around ten I go out, to Le Bar for a change. I bring a guy back, some preppy, totally tired and anti-sex, but truly very handsome. As expected, I fuck him. As expected, it's terrible.

The day after around noon Terrier calls. I tell him what's up. He says he wants to see me. I say OK since Stéphane is not around. I do not sleep out ever. That's the rule. Other than that I have the right to do as I please. So here at home it's OK. He arrives on time. I'd offered to take him out to eat but changed my mind late in the afternoon and, without letting him know, went to

Dubernet and bought treats to eat. I got young partridge terrine and brioches with foie gras, and I made a small salad on the side. We drink burgundy. After coffee I starting feeling a serious need for sex. I back up against the kitchen cupboards with my pelvis thrust forward to make him salivate over my half-hard dick under my old 501s. He puts up a fuss but I eventually get him down on all fours sucking me there and then it's really quite nice, he loses consciousness of everything else, it lasts a long time the way I like, he drools so much it runs down my balls and down his chin, I bend down to kiss him, I feel it driving him crazy, I break away, I bring him into the bathroom to wash out his ass and then we go to the bedroom and I fuck him long and really to the core, I go in and out, I ram him as far as it goes, he huffs and puffs like grandpa, twists up his face, he's wearing a goatee these days and it looks really good on him because he's got such a beautiful mouth, he's entirely scrunched up under me, it's so much better than with Stéphane but I don't care for now. I look him straight in the eye and ram him harder and harder and then he shuts his eyes and screams and shoots big jets of cum without touching his dick, and I come out and I hose him down with mine.

The day after, operation day, I have an enormous amount of work and I can't go see Stéphane. I call him when he's up to let him know I'll come by the next day. I think about Quentin's operation last December. In no time he'd begun fucking again. He would cruise the Minitel with one hand. He would fuck and get fucked with the dildo. He'd do it on his back the first few days to keep from having to move his upper body. Every day I would wash him, I'd untie and tie back up the thing he had to wear, a sort of shirt-sling. I would feed him. I would dress him. I would bathe him. It was cool. We had quite a few orgies through it all. Once he was no longer in need of me we had grown apart again.

The following day I still have a thousand things to deal with. I'm running too late for the time I said, but I can't bring myself to call I feel so guilty. I arrive at the hospital at seven-thirty. I'm supposed to have dinner with my father at eight-thirty. By the time I locate the correct wing of the hospital, then the room (I've forgotten the room number, there isn't anyone anymore anywhere to ask), it's going on eight. Stéphane is asleep. I watch him awhile. He wakes up. We talk. I caress his hand. I'm astonished by the flowers in the room. As a rule it's forbidden, there's the risk of infection. It was his ex who came to see him earlier in the day who brought them. I talk to him about things that passed through my mind during my hospital stay a year ago. I tell him I saw Terrier and I couldn't help fucking. He says he's not surprised. He asks me about Terrier. The eye that's not covered in a bloodstained bandage looks at me sad when he tells me he was thinking I wasn't going to come at all.

A few days later Terrier calls around three in the afternoon. He asks me You wouldn't know what time it is, would you? Voice very very hoarse. I say Why, you don't have a watch? No, I broke it. I say It's three o'clock.

He says Ah OK and you wouldn't know what day it is? I say Friday why? He says Ugh I wanted to know if it's been three days or four days I've been asleep. Way to go! I say, and how did you swing that? Simple. After making the rounds of the pharmacies where he got nothing, he slashed his wrists and then he stopped the blood and took sleeping pills. So how do you feel? I say. All right, he says, except I'm a little hungry. I'll be over right away, I say. I tear myself out of the apartment, I go by the supermarket where he lives, I buy coke, bio apple juice, cheese, saucisson, canned spinach, Nestlé milk, grated carrots, pain de campagne, endives, smoked salmon, butter, yoghurt, little jars of baby food (vegetable-lamb and apple-banana, they have no apple-quince), and the newspapers.

I arrive, he lets me in, all white in the white warm-up pants I gave him. On me they're tight, ultra-provoca-tive, on him less so, but he's still just as hot. I eat a bite of celery rémoulade and then some saucisson. I insist he eat some of the baby food. I make him open the bed, we take a little nap, he shows me pictures of his parents' and grandparents' weddings, I make comments. We talk, kiss each other, pick on each other, he tells me that during his stay in the country he had Frédéric, a friend of my mother's, so I find out that Frédéric has a very nice thick eight-inch dick. He sucked it and then he said We should stop, we don't have condoms. But it's Frédéric's friend he really wants, and also Frédéric's friend's boyfriend. Terrier is really a tramp just like me. Ah yes, I also brought him over the jar of green plum preserves I put up myself and that I was supposed to give him a month ago, a jar crammed with fruits that were plump like mushrooms, a jar with a red lid. I yell at him about his attempted suicide. Well what do you expect? he says to me. You never come by to see me, you never return my messages. You're only interested in me when I'm not doing well. I was really touched you didn't eat my preserves or give them away to somebody else. They were for him, I tell him. At the end we go out and buy cigarettes, he walks me back to the métro.

6 DIVERSIONS

I wake at four in the afternoon, having fallen asleep
around seven in the morning after fucking some prick
I'd brought back from the QG only because he was the
first passable guy to hook up with me. The evening had
been horrible, I was having no success at all. Try as I
did to convince myself there were too many hot guys
that night and that's what kills the ambience, I still felt
like a piece of shit, like I didn't exist. A guy I knew was
there, someone Stéphane and I had previously hooked
up with. I'd been feeling up his ass through his leather
pants and I told him I didn't feel much of anything. He
undid his belt for me to feel things better. I put my hand
in, put my index finger on his ass, which had a past, I
fondled his hole, he dropped his drawers, I fingered his
ass in full view of the whole bar, he was peacefully
sniffing poppers, which got me hard. I'd put his hand
on my crotch. Proposed we go to my place. No
response. He went back downstairs to the backroom. I
was enraged he'd brush me off like that. I followed him,
found him opening a condom to fuck some guy in a

corner nook. I stayed to watch, looking focused, concentrating. Ordinarily nobody approaches me in backrooms because I don't look interested enough. I think it's pointless, in fact, all this fiddling around. At best a quick sodomy standing up. Yuk. But there I was watching him real hard, really hoping it would unbalance him. And then the guy next to me started in with his hands. I did it back to him. We kept it up. My enemy stopped fucking. This was pleasure, I told myself. I had thrown him off balance. I felt a little avenged.

Like an idiot I carried on with the other guy. The moment he turned towards the wall and began wanking faster I was so depressed I said How about we finish up at my place? He asked Where is your place? Round the corner, I answered. I knew there was no point in bringing him home, but I didn't have the courage to go home alone. Once we got home we fucked of course. When I had my hand almost in his ass, he started saying Oh yeah oh man, your hand in my ass, oh yeah I like that, kind of as if he was dubbing a porn movie. I checked his dick. He wasn't hard. It disgusted me. Plus he wanted to see me again.

I woke up super-sleazed. I got on the Minitel almost immediately. There was nothing other than a guy I'd made contact with a few times already. He re-contacted me with a plan involving Es and ladies' panties. I knew he was a tired thing, Quentin had told me, he'd done him last year, but whatever, there was nothing else and I wasn't really up to going out and searching for something better so I said OK. He called me back to propose the same plan but as a three-way, with a young guy he knew, twenty-seven, good-looking, versatile. I said OK, naturally.

They arrived toward the end of the afternoon. The young guy looked good. The one I knew already was, as expected, tired. Totally out of it, must have been on his second or third E of the day, plus his thing was shit drugs, he palmed some off on me for double the going rate, actually he was a dealer of shit drugs. He didn't get hard. We took care of business between us, Eric and I. Then the old troll left. It was cool. Early still. We had all our time before Stéphane would come home, he was coming back very late after a meeting. It was good for me I thought to fuck a guy my own age. I passed him my leather chaps. They made his buns firecrackers. Every time he would turn around I'd be fixated, they were so plump, so curved, white and round. Like mammy's titties.

He didn't know how to do anything except suck, piss and fist. But these I have to say he did very well, his eyes wide open watching, and with a hard-on. First I sucked him. After that he worked over my ass. He was very precise, I was hard without touching myself, his hand went up to his wrist in my ass, I verified how deep in the mirror. I felt myself coming. I asked him to come out quick. I came. He said I'm all excited. I asked How come? He said Because I had a hard-on and I didn't touch myself all the time I was fisting you. I said It's normal, you did it right, that's why, when I used to give my ex the dildo it would always give me a raging hard-on. I rolled another joint. Then I took care of him. I used the riding crop, one hand was holding his cock, small precise strokes harder and harder, on the top, then the sides, then the balls softer, then back to the dick. He had a mean hard-on. I gave him my cock to suck, he gave great head. My rod was heavy and pliable, thick, what you have when you've already been doing stuff for an hour or two. We kept it up.

He forgot and left his poppers at my place. He called the next day to tell me. I told him it was classic. He said With you, everything's classic. That made me laugh. On second thought, I could have told him it was simply a matter of statistics. He told me he hasn't done a lot of fucking. In my world, a lot of fucking, that means more than three men a week. What I do these days. Quentin had done a lot before he met me himself. And after too. There was a time he would have a regular and different guy for each night of the week, weekends he would leave open for newcomers. Fucking is always better with regulars. The problem is the relationships you have to manage. But Quentin is borderline schizophrenic, so this doesn't bother him. When nobody exists really, there's room for everybody. I wonder if I am like him. I don't believe I am, but I'm not so sure.

7 IT'S STARTING AGAIN

The next day's Monday. We go out to dinner, Stéphane
and I, the Diable des Lombards. I love this place. It's the
Ritz of the ghetto. Plus, now that I am old I always run
into acquaintances. This evening it's a tall one, the model
type but not bad, we had given our number at a restaurant three months before. He'd left a message a week
later, but it was vacation time, we'd left him a message
saying we were going away. When we got back we didn't
call him, things had cooled down too much. I hook up
with him again as I go past, getting up from my table.
Worth watching. We go for a final drink at the QG. We
run into a friend I've already had two or three real hot
times with, the Doc I call him because he's a doctor.
We bring him home. It's nearly already an hour we've
been fucking, Stéphane, the Doc and I, when the doorbell rings. Shit, I say to myself. It has to be Terrier. We
come to a halt. Then, nothing more. I begin cleaning
out Stéphane again. Stéphane begins blowing the Doc
again. The Doc begins with Stéphane's nipples again.
The doorbell rings again. This ring has got to be his. I

pull out of the ass. I keep the condom on to go let him in, to show him that dropping in on people at three-thirty in the morning is not done. But it doesn't work at all because when I open the door he falls in through the doorway, he's completely tanked. How much did you have to drink? A bottle of scotch. I look down at the dirty carpet by the entryway. He says I want to sleep here. I say You are sickening, really you are sickening. I leave him. The other two are still in the bedroom. I give them the low-down. They quiet me down. I go back to Terrier. OK, you can sleep in the guest room. Since he won't budge, I drag him into the room and I shut the door.

Afterwards it is impossible to get back into fucking because instead of sleeping he stalks around the apartment. We joke that we ought to tie him up to the radiator and fuck in front of him, that would be fun at least. And then I hear sliding, the door to the medicine cabinet in the bathroom. When I get there he looks content. Immediately I look for the Lexomil prescription I'd just bought. The bottle is empty. The little fucker has come to my place to commit suicide. It's the third fake attempt in two weeks. The last time at least was at his place. All right. I yank him by the collar and I drag him like a kitten towards the toilet. Hey! What do you think you're doing Guillaume? Have you lost it? No no I haven't lost it. It's you who's lost it. But when we get to the toilet, he will not agree to puke. I'm sure if I cram two fingers down his throat he'll bite me. I let it go. I leave him there, collapsed on the floor. The others are still in the bedroom. I don't know what to do, I say. What did he take? A bottle of scotch and a prescription of Lexomil. Well that's not enough to kill him, he's just going to be sleeping for three or four days. But I don't want him sleeping three or four days in my place when I'm not here. He's done this on purpose, he knows I'm going away tomorrow, I told him today on the phone. I ask the Doc what you normally do in such a situation. The Doc says that in such a situation you call the rescue squad, you stop washing your dirty laundry in private, when he comes to in the emergency ward he'll understand that this is serious.

I call the rescue squad. I'm buzzed, we've smoked two fat joints, done a maximum of poppers, I'm afraid my voice gives this away. Hello, bonsoir Monsieur, I have someone at my place who's just tried to commit suicide. What did the person use? A prescription of Lexomil and a bottle of scotch. They give me a hard time about coming to get him. I say I don't have a car, I can't bring him to the Hôtel-Dieu. OK they're on their way. We begin getting him dressed. He resists as much as he can. The Doc wishes us luck, says he'll be running along. We look more or less normal when the paramedics arrive, at least I think we do. They don't seem especially enchanted about being here. Come on now, monsieur, you've got to get up now, no no, no sleeping here, c'mon, let's get dressed now. Stéphane and I finish dressing him. His boots, why bother?

Yes indeed, this Terrier is one organised boy. In his little pocket is his orange métro card, his identity card, his Social Security card, some money. Phew. They cart him down the stairs in a chair. I go behind. See you later. In the van next to the stretcher I freak, they must think we're a bunch of dirty depraved faggots I think, and then I say to myself Well actually they must be more used to this kind of thing than I am. The streets pass in the windows of the van.

At the Hôtel-Dieu there are bums looking for some place to sleep and being thrown out, and there are plenty of cops. I'm still real buzzed. They unload Terrier. Male nurses, female nurses. They bring him in on the stretcher. The head nurse, a brunette, looks accusing when she sends me to register my friend. I go across the sleeping hospital. The admission room's small cubicles are all empty. The black gentleman is kind. I ask him how many suicide attempts there are each night on average. He says Oh misfortunes like that we see a lot of.

I returned to Emergency to hand over the papers. I asked what was going to happen. The nurse told me they were going to pump his stomach and I'd have to wait. So I waited. I knew there was nothing to wait for but I couldn't leave. I heard Terrier scream out my name very loud. There was a noisy metallic sound. A nurse rushed around. I went to the desk. I asked the nurse if there was a problem, but she didn't have the time to answer because the head nurse had arrived. They spoke in low voices. Then the head nurse turned toward me and said You're Guillaume? I didn't dare lie. I nodded.

He's asking for you, she said. He wants to see you. I think it's better he doesn't, I said.

I waited some more, totally paranoid from the joint that still wouldn't go away. Plus every half-hour tons of cops would pull up with guys who were bleeding more or less. Terrier rolled by whiter than the sheet on his gurney, asleep at last, a drip in his arm. I was told that I could call him around noon, when he'd be awake. I walked all the way home. I got undressed in the hallway and then I went into the bedroom and when I sat down on the bed Stéphane woke up and I told him what had happened and held him in my arms as usual and we fell asleep.

I saw Terrier again some time later. Stéphane was away in the country at his parents. As usual, I tried to fuck him. He didn't want to. I told Stéphane I thought Terrier was right about this. Him and me fucking didn't do him any good.

8 PARTY TIME

I put up some preserves for two or three days, then I finally agreed to go away with Stéphane for the weekend of the eleventh because it was with a group of friends and we were going off to London.

Clubbers are the most civilised of all people. The most difficult. They pay more attention to their conduct than an aristocrat in a salon. You don't talk about obvious things at night. You don't talk about work, about money, about books, about records, about movies. You only act. Speech is action. The eye on the lookout. The gesture charged with meaning. Clubland. All over the planet. Tonight we're in London. I recommend the *ff* for the drugs, truly for the connoisseur. They're there as well. La créme de la créme. The most beautiful, the chicest, the toughest in the world. The club is full. We each take half an E I have left over, but it's not enough for bearing the music here. Too hardcore. I go look around for something more after I've rolled and smoked a joint in a corner of the bar.

In a space by a pillar there's a guy bending over a

little spoon somebody else is holding. I go stand next to them, not too near. I wait for them to finish. The one sniffing goes off. Are you selling anything, I ask the other one? No, he goes. Do you know anyone selling anything? He says I'll go see if I see someone I know. I'll be back in a minute. He comes back five minutes later with a tall bodybuilder in a torso harness. The bodybuilder takes me to the other end of the bar. The dealer is big and black and very sexy. How much for an E? Fifteen. And for acid? Five. The E is the most expensive yet, but it's got to be better here. I only have ten quid on me, so I buy two hits of acid. We each do a half, Stéphane and I. I go back to see the dealer though, and buy two Es for later.

After a joint I manage to dance even to hardcore, a little frustrated though because the rhythm is too simple for me to do what I like. Besides, all the butchos in leather are bad dancers with few exceptions, the ones on so much speed they are able to follow the rhythm. I dance none the less in the near-darkness at the back of the club. The floor is wet, slippery to the max. It is so hot I'm drenched in sweat in one minute. Cool. It warms up my dick. With the drugs I'd almost forgotten about it. Afterwards I'm out of breath, I go chill on the edge of the dance floor. I don't know where Stéphane is. Anyway he doesn't dance, he has a complex about that too.

I begin to get real bored. I go thank the guy who gave me the drug tip. You never know. And then, for the principle also. He's still in the same spot. I say Thanks for the tip. He flashes me an enormous trendy smile. I locate Stéphane. I'm full of hate for this place. This music is lousy. The people are too snobby. The mega-butch bodybuilder who touched my crotch when I went by him a while ago is still glaring at me with these avid eyes devoid of any expression. He works my nerves. I tell Stéphane I can't stand these people any more. I only like people who know there's more to it than just themselves. Plus, here there's nothing but asses patiently waiting for the dick they know they're cute enough to get for real. It works my nerves.

The bodybuilder passes by again. Five-seven, one hundred and seventy-five pounds minimum of muscle. Shaved head. Not a hair on his body. Enormous tits, one is pierced with a big chrome ring. Such a lady, I say. I look at him, not in a nice way, I think. He stops half the way up the flight of stairs. My expression pleases him apparently.

I've had enough. I propose to Stéphane we get going, the place closes in half an hour anyway, might as well avoid the queue at the coat-check. I pick up mine. Put it on. Stéphane waits for his. I chill, leaning against the security gate that bars the entrance. He's there. He comes up to me. His pupils really ultra-dilated. I want you to fuck me, he growls out with this great Cockney accent. I look at him. I'm like Sure. He says to me Come on. With your boyfriend. I say OK. I search for Stéphane. We go back down the stairs. Now there's a queue for the coat-check. The men's room is full. We go to the Ladies. A stall opens. I'd already noticed the girl coming out, brown hair with a white top trimmed in black. She smiles at us, as trashed as we are. We enter. We strip to the minimum, pants at ankles. He has the head of his dick pierced, he doesn't get hard. He sucks us. When we are exploitable he takes out his condoms. They use ultra-thick condoms here, but it's all right, I'm hard. I fuck him. He's tense and stiff, his ass is a little too high. I get in anyway without any gel, thank you acid. The trouble is it's uncomfortable and I don't feel much of anything. I pass him to Stéphane. Stéphane shoves it in. This turns me back on. He passes him back to me, etc., etc. We eventually lose what hard-ons we have. He wants us to shoot our wads on him. You feel like shooting your wad on him, I say to Stéphane? Stéphane's like Not really. Me neither, I say, I don't want to waste it, I'd prefer something back at the hotel with the usual. And so we don't shoot our wads. I think it'll be OK like this, I say. We button up. He says I'm sure I'll see you around sometimes guys. His politeness works my nerves. Where? I say. Do you often make it to Paris? He's like No. Then it's not so sure, I say.

When we get out the Indian taxi driver who throws himself on us staggers so much on the way to his cab we come back to the door and get another driver, a black apparently sober. He listens to disco. Cool. We pass milk lorries in the enormous streets of the deserted city. The black drives good and fast. You're a smooth driver, I say to him, I like that. He's like Oh.

I want Stéphane to fuck me wearing the latex hood, a one-piece, holes only for nostrils I bought at the Clone

Zone this afternoon. On acid I know it'll be great. He agrees. He fucks me. Two times in a row he fucks me, the bed makes a racket out of hell, and then he fists me. I come three times, him once, at the end. Lexomil to cut the acid, and sleep. Joint. The atmosphere is still thick though.

The day after, I want to look hot. I shave, and leave a goatee to make my mouth an asset. I give myself real long sideburns. Black leather pants. A rocker's belt. Rangers. Tight tight bright red T-shirt with silver stars cut to show the hairs around my navel and a slight protruding belly. Top class. I share an E with Stéphane for the depression. It's not working between us. I ditched him once already last week. I realise I've been trying for some time now to replace him. Yesterday I asked Sandrine, a friend who lives here, if she had a boyfriend. She told me No, I'm alone. I'm waiting for something good. It's all right to be alone too. I said Yeah I agree. I thought me too, I should be alone, waiting.

At Substation, the evening got off to a pretty dreary start. Not many people. We did the two Es we got from *ff*. I got off progressively, very strong but mellow. I began dancing by the pinball machine Stéphane was playing with le grand Christophe. Then the dance floor. There I came to realise I had just taken the best E of my life. I danced like I hadn't danced in a long time. Like I never had actually. Less repetitive. Freer. More choreographic. I jumped in the air more than a few times. At the end of the night I even did a few spinarounds, ten times, one after the other. Great DJ. The best set I ever heard I believe, the most happy and deep house, bigger than life really. There was one moment in particular (it must have been two or three already, the place was closing at four) when I looked over at the DJ so he would look back at me. I gave him the thumbs up. He did the same. I danced, and a tall guy leaned over and said I like you, I pray to God you'll stay alive. This kind of threw me, but I still said Thank you.

A little skinhead was dancing real hot, kind of excited. We were the two best dancers on the floor once the one or two girls who were there at the beginning had gone. We were watching each other, appreciating each other. At one point when his back was close to me, I caught him up and made like I was fucking him. It felt good to hold his tight muscly hips. Then I turned around and it was his turn. He made bang bang bang bang bang right there on the floor. We kissed for a long time. Stéphane had run off somewhere. Some nipple squeezing. I touched him, the small of his back, his lower body, I put a finger on the top of his crack, he felt soft. I touched him exactly like he could have been mine. Stéphane had come back. I pulled away a few inches and said I have a boyfriend. Where is he? he said. He's here, I said and showed him Stéphane. Don't play around with love if you've got a boyfriend, he said. Or you'll get a punch in your face. And then he left me alone with Stéphane. Stéphane went off again. I went and bought a beer although as a rule I don't mix E and alcohol.

It was closing time. I queued up at the coat-check.

The little skinhead was coming and going, yelling Everybody's counting his money! But I want some flesh! And nobody will give me a shag! Just because I'm a gay national star! I asked the black guy in front of me Is he really the star he says he is? No, he's just the contrary, the black answered. He's what we call in English a complete asshole. I thought he was saying that out of jealousy.

Stéphane goes to sleep as soon as we get in, to forget about me. It's four a.m. We could be fucking. I wank. It's great. This really was the best night out though. Don't play around with love if you've got a boyfriend.

When we got back from London I told Stéphane I was leaving him. He told me it didn't surprise him. He went out to do the rounds of the bars. I wanked. It was great. And then I listened to one of the house compilations I'd bought over there. After that I listened to Propaganda, Duel.

I thought about Eric P who knew how to choose music so well, and who always felt like jumping out whenever he went near a window after he'd been smoking.

I wouldn't be surprised if he killed me. If he had a revolver.

9 SEPARATION

Stéphane said he'd leave the apartment at the end of the week. I'm glad he's not leaving right now. But it's not very amusing between us. We hardly speak to each other. Sometimes we cry. We sleep without touching each other. Finally he leaves for a week at his parents. We call each other. I say that I don't know any more, I need distance, if we continue seeing each other it must be under the best conditions, I have to hurt him less, I have to feel better. When he comes back he's going to stay with a friend. He moves out while I'm at work. I look for a studio or a one-bedroom. I eventually find something a little out of the way but not so bad. I pack my cartons.

On moving day morning a guy who'd hooked up with me two months earlier on the Minitel called me on the phone offering to give me a piercing. I asked if we couldn't see each other toward the end of the week. He said he was free that afternoon only, after that he was going away. I said OK come by. I had thought about this a long time. Lots of guys I saw or knew had had it done.

Not I. It was one of the only things I hadn't done already. But now I felt like doing something serious. Plus he was the one who had made the initial contact. Interested in a piercing? Yes, I'd answered, but what of, if not the face, not the tits, not the dick? That leaves the navel, the perineum, the sack, he'd typed in. The sack? The balls, he'd replied. Why not? I'd typed. He said he would call.

He arrived at the empty apartment with his small case, a little late because he'd just re-pierced a guy he'd pierced the year before. He was very tall, wide shoulders, pretty ugly and badly dressed. We chatted over a glass of water. He showed me his piercings, the two nipples, the one on the right had two rings, he'd added one recently. I asked him if it was healing properly. He said Yes, only you have to disinfect it regularly because it gets a little puffy. He squeezed for pus to come out.

We chatted for a long time because I wanted to be sure I could trust him. He showed me his material. He told me we'd begin when I felt ready. In a while I said I thought we could get on with it. I settled down on the front room sofa, the only stick of furniture left in the apartment. He gave me anaesthetic in the scrotum. We waited. It was still sensitive. I asked him to give me a second shot. We waited. My scrotum was puffing up. It was still sensitive. I said that I didn't want to feel any pain, I wanted more anaesthesia. He told me he'd never seen that before. There's a first time for everything, I said. I thought he might not have minded actually if I'd had a rough time. He gave me a third shot. We waited. I talked to lighten up the atmosphere. I pinched myself. I wasn't feeling anything any more. It's OK now we can go on, I said. We went into the bathroom, for the blood. I sat on the edge of the tub. He pulled on my balls, placed surgical clamps on either side of the sack. I was watching. He began to pierce, a needle about two and a half to three inches long with a placement loop fixed at the end. The needle went through, then the loop. He had a hard time screwing shut the little closing ball because the blood was making his latex gloves slip. He disinfected it. I held the bandage because there was bleeding.

He made a call on his mobile. Another piercing. A nipple I believe. He left. I waited for Stéphane. He was supposed to come help me transport some stuff. The bleeding wasn't stopping. Stéphane arrived late, looking tremendously happy to see me. I told him there was a problem, I'd just got my balls pierced and the bleeding wasn't stopping. He said But how long does this mean we're not going to be able to fuck? I said Two, three weeks. He groaned as if I'd struck him. He banged his fist against the wall. I realised I'd just blown our new departure.

I stuffed toilet paper down my jockey shorts. The blood was beginning to spot my 501s. We took his car. He drove me to my apartment. He brought up the things I had with me. I tried not to move too much, for the haemorrhaging to stop. He stayed a while and

then he went home to sleep, he had to get up early
the next day.

10 THE NIGHT BEFORE CHRISTMAS

For Christmas I was alone in the new apartment. My bank account had been devastated by the move, I'd had to work hard to bring in the dough. As soon as I had finished I got sick. Stéphane came by and brought me ham and canned soup before he went away to his parents. We were supposed to go see a painting exhibition that was ending, the one time he was free a weekday afternoon. And then I was sick. Both of us thought without saying so that this was really the end. He didn't stay long.

I called my mother to tell her we still could get together as a family, which was slightly phoney: had she offered I'd have refused. I was thinking about Quentin. Our first year we'd ended up one inside the other the evening of the twenty-fourth. He had smiled above me. Joyeux Noël mon chéri. We had kissed. For New Year's eve, same thing. It was now three years we hadn't respected the tradition.

I sat down in front of the Minitel screen. I hooked up with a guy whose pseudonym was Fuck No Condom.

The little Minitel guy asked me what in his CV had attracted me. I answered Fucking you without a condom. I thought he was suspicious. Safe sex isn't spelled out in my CV, but it's true I do have the CV of a guy who practises safe sex. Guys who fuck without condoms never go into detail about what kind of fucking they practise, hard or soft or raunch or man-to-man or whatever other nuance, wallowing in the poisoned cum is what interests them in fact, it is romantic and dark fucking, I'm saying this in a condescending way, but this much is true: it is very strong. One time in a three-way I kept losing my hard-on in their asses, and when they fucked me I was too freaked having unsafe sex. OK, we don't know anything about reinfection but we do know that with this kind of thing we can catch a lot more crap. Even so, when the little nasty guy with no condom shot off in the tall skinhead's ass it was breathtaking. The kiss of death they say.

When he called me he said he was more into fucking than getting fucked tonight. Here's one that's not stupid, I thought. I said I think there's going to be a problem then because I don't get fucked without a condom. He told me he wasn't going to come over. We didn't have the same despair. I promised myself that when my T4s fall below two hundred I would start.

I took the remaining E from the fridge and got off sticking stuff up my ass in front of some porn movie I passed my time rewinding. I was so high I knocked down the Christmas tree and the CD tower when I was manipulating my sack of dildos. That was funny I thought.

11 MERRY CHRISTMAS!

I woke around one. I wasn't hungry, feeling fit, still buzzed from the E. I drank just a glass of water and sat down at the Minitel. I connected with a guy who had a friendly sounding program: reciprocal fucking, Jeff Stryker dildos. Everything went as planned except after we'd got our asses opened good with the Strykers he'd brought, we were standing up again, I offered his big, glistening, greasy, no-condom dick my ass. He slid in me. It felt good. He soon came to a stop. I turned him around, my turn to slide in. Then back to the dildo. I shoved the Stryker deep inside him and fucked him with it while I sat back down on his big purple dick. Then he did the same thing to me. We came one after the other, dildos in to the bottom of both of us. I told myself since there hadn't been any semen in anybody's ass, this was more or less all right.

That evening I had dinner in the Marais, at a friend's who for years would invite us regularly to dinner, Quentin and me. I'd also been to his place once with Stéphane. I arrived on time. We had a drink before dinner with his current boyfriend. I said that I'd just split up with Stéphane. We had dinner. After that I found myself out in the cold of the streets. It must have been around one. I wondered whether I should go home, sleep, get some rest, or else go out. I decided you need to have faith in life, Christmas must be the right time for that. I walked in the night to the Quetzal. I thought there'd be an interesting crowd, the hardcore waifs without a family. There were indeed quite a few. I got a beer, I posted myself where you have the best visibility, there at the door to the toilets. I inspected the merchandise. I was perfectly detached. Even if there wasn't anything, OK. I was willing to go home without waiting to be asked twice.

There was nothing extraordinary. And then I saw this tall black guy in a cap. I mean tall. Six-foot fourish, two hundred and forty pounds, great big and strapping, on the heavy side, young, a very handsome face. He looked reserved. We exchanged smiles. I went over and I said to him Where are you from in America? He said I'm not from America, I'm from Africa. I said Oh OK so you must be some sort of African prince.

This made him laugh. We spoke about him, about me, about Zen. His hotel was in the Etoile. We went to my place.

At home instead of grabbing him immediately, I started rolling a joint stretched out on the bed. He didn't want to smoke. He asked me if I smoked all the time. No, I said, only every evening. So you're a druggy, he said. Which I denied. I smoked my joint.

We weren't fucking. He did get undressed though because the heat was up full blast. He was lying next to me in his T-shirt and underwear. I asked him if he wouldn't mind if I sucked him. You can try if you really want to, he said. Five minutes later he did have a hard-on after all. I slipped a condom on him and I sat down on his pointy, very big dick. He wasn't making a move. We weren't kissing. I was fucking myself. In a while he turned me around and rammed me very quick and very hard, almost without touching me. I had to brainwash myself, had to keep repeating to myself that I was just a little white whore getting screwed by a big black man, just so I would be able to keep my hard-on and then come the same time as him no less. I have to say he took his time about it. I had all the time anybody would need. I asked him afterwards if he didn't usually use his hands more when fucking. He said he did. I thought this over.

12 NEGOTIATIONS

Quentin calls me. He tells me things are going bad
between him and Nico. I say You don't love him anyway.
At least I dumped Stéphane. He says I want to see you.
You don't want to come over? I say Are you serious?
With that boyfriend of yours dragging his tired ass in at
any moment? Fucking no way. He says We can meet up
at the Quetzal then. Going out now seems completely
beyond me, plus totally useless. And then I want him to
be the one to make the effort. He's the one looking
to get me back after all. I say No I'm not going out. You
can come over here. He says OK I'll be there in an hour.
I know he needs at least an hour and a half, if you take
into account the joints plus the Xanax. He told me he
had decreased the dosage. I don't know if this is true.
He lies all the time. Two hours pass and I understand
that there's a problem. I check at his place. Machine. I
speak in case he's screening. No answer. He calls a
couple of minutes later. My building code isn't working.
I say OK I'll come down. I throw on some jeans no
underwear, my bomber jacket with no T-shirt, hi-tops

with no socks. Downstairs nobody. The code works fine. I wait five minutes. I tell myself he must have got the wrong street. I run in the rain to the same street number as mine on the Faubourg St-Denis. I think about a four-way we did four years ago a few doors down, at a place with these two guys, superb tall hunky versatile guys, great big dicks both of them. They had a huge chunk of excellent hash. Everybody had fucked me but it was Quentin they obviously preferred, with him there were more things they could do. I wound up with a big dildo in my ass, which wasn't a habit of mine at the time. It was too much. Quentin told me the day after that he'd woken up with one of them in him fucking him.

Nobody. I go back home. Time interminable passes, it seems, and then the telephone rings. I say You got the street wrong. It's not St-Denis, it's St-Martin. I hang up. He arrives, totally out of it. He criticises the apartment everybody thinks is great except my sister and me. I say I know all this. It's all I could afford. He rolls a joint that to me looks fat. We bring up the past. He has changed, he explains to me. We bring up our possible future. I tell him I want to fuck now, so we'll know where we stand. He says No, he thinks it's too early yet, maybe later, at his New Year party, where there'll be coke and no Nico, who has to spend it with his parents out in the provinces.

After a while he asks me to come sit on his lap. I'm not too keen on this but I go sit there anyway. Installed there stiff as a marionette, I compare this with the effect it had on me in the old days. We kiss. It's perfect technically, but it doesn't get me hard. Eventually he leaves. I go on the Minitel and since that isn't working I go to a fuck bar.

When I arrived there was practically nobody. A young hard body was lying there waiting, his legs apart, his ankles in the stirrups of a sling, a big hard dick, naked entirely except for a pair of marine-blue Converse hitops he was wearing without socks. I went into the booth in the back. I waited. Two monsters poked a head in. I made a face. They left. A half-hour I was there.

Nothing was up. I came out of the booth. I went around. He was still in the big sling. I went in front of him. I began to jerk off. It turned me on to think he was there to get fucked by just anybody. I pressed my dick against his hole. I said I don't have a condom. He said That's all right. I lubricated with spit. I had a hard time entering. And then I did. I fucked him with finesse. He stayed hard without touching himself. A guy arrived. He came up close to see. Instinctively I plastered myself up against the guy's ass to keep the other guy from seeing we were fucking without a condom. He saw though. He left. I kept on. I felt myself coming. I asked myself Do I come in him? That's what he wants anyway. And then I came out and shot off on the floor. I returned to my booth. I ended up with a dick, then a dildo, then a fist, a real hot little guy who worked me over like a god and who was saying to me That's right man, go ahead, let me see those eyes roll back in your head.

13 AND A HAPPY NEW YEAR!

I arrived at Quentin's at ten past midnight. The guests weren't completely through kissing. I inspected the apartment where none of the necessary work had been done since my departure. Quentin was drug-fucked. Coke I thought, but also joint after joint he was extorting from a poor girl clinging to his coat-tails although I was sure he had his own stash. An hour passed and still there was no talk of the coke he'd told me about the night before. Because I'd had enough waiting for him to be polite, I went and asked him for it. I said I'd prefer not to have to do this, but since you're not offering I must ask. Where's that coke? He said How much you give me for it? I said Not one thing, you kidding or what. I'm not about to pay you for a line of coke. He said Oh all right. He made off. I waited. Finally he came and told me to take the yellow straw in the pot on the mantle in the bedroom and join him in the bathroom. In the bathroom there was also Nico who'd just arrived and said how great it was to be together again after a year. I wanted to kill him but I kept my trap shut for the coke.

I simply released his arm from around my shoulders that was really too much.

The coke was shitty, rough and freaky. Or else it was the party. I had jolts of energy nevertheless. Danced some. From time to time Quentin would look at me, high and also enamoured. Then Nico would come by for reassurance. Well of course we're going to fuck and sleep together, says Quentin, go cut us an E in half, the first one didn't do much. Nico came back to say he wasn't able, he didn't know how, there were too many people in the kitchen. Quentin yelled at him. I was disgusted. Can't you see he just wants some attention? He didn't answer. He did not budge.

I danced some more, without conviction. Had a discussion with some stars from the ghetto I did not like and who did not like me either. At around two, a terribly hot one arrived, a truly monstrous beauty, very young. He swept in front of me for the toilet. When he came out I couldn't resist, I had to talk to him. I said You're David aren't you? He said No I'm Ivan. Ah, I said, then you're not the dealer everybody's waiting for. He said No I'm not him, David's supposed to drop by though, I saw him a little while ago at another party. I thought This one is truly perfect. He said I don't have a lot of energy tonight. I said Go lie down or else do some drugs. He said I did some coke already but I haven't got any pep. I asked him his age to know how old you have to be to have skin like his. Twenty-one he said. He's one of the ones kept by a real famous clothes designer, Quentin told me later. They're all a little band of marvels like him, they go to the gym every day, the sun booth every day, do drugs every day. They don't do anything, they're sponsored. All of them between eighteen and twenty-two.

Two hours on and I was beginning to wilt. I was sitting next to him reading some pathetic thing he had written and wanted to show me. This nice little guy who was playing records all night leaned over to me and said You look sad. I looked up. I thought he was making a pass, and it worked me because I hadn't even looked at him before, and now I was thinking he wasn't bad and I told myself that I was thinking this only because he was cruising me and then I said Well I do have the right don't I? It was dumb. Nico was hovering around us, dying of jealousy. A while ago, for the first time since he's known me, he proposed me his big bundle. He apparently sensed Quentin was after me again, his ass was scared. It is true I've always ached for his nine inches, but his offer came too late.

Three hours on I saw myself in a mirror and I looked washed out, grey, dead. I asked Quentin How can you stand it? He said It's hard. I got on my coat and left. I walked as far as the canal, Place Stalingrad, there was next to nobody, I hung around anyway, spoke with a guy done up in a riot-police uniform. I got in bed at six. The next day I woke with a fever.

Quentin called me two days later. He wanted a favour, he had to come over to explain. I received him in a bathrobe. He held out a small blue package. Gift. I said Thanks, and put it aside unopened. He lit a cigarette without asking. I pointed out to him that this might bother me. I began to insult him, for Nico, for me, for his perpetual lack of clarity, his ill treatment of people. I thrust the package he'd brought me back into the pocket of his bomber jacket. I threw him out. He called the next day to tell me this hurt him but it was delicious, no doubt, to be tortured by the one you love. I couldn't bring myself to believe him one split second. I told myself This time it's over.

14 BITES

A few days later I was doing better. I went back to the Quetzal. I saw friends. We caught up. Dennis got around to telling me he was worried, waiting for the results of his test because he'd been doing stupid shit. I said What kind of stupid shit? He said Well last year I was with a guy for a few months and we were fucking without condoms. I said Ahh. He said And I just now found out he's sick. I said Yes that is scary. He said not only that but he was still unemployed, he didn't get the job he was hoping for. To change the atmosphere I asked him which of the guys there he'd had were a good fuck, although I didn't have much confidence in him for this kind of thing, in my opinion our criteria were not similar, but it was four years since I'd fucked him, he might have made progress.

He pointed out a little guy our age, maybe slightly younger, shaved head, tight white T-shirt, hard body, quite star-like, talking with some girls also rather star-like ten feet from us. He said There's him, you'd get along fine with him I'm sure. I said Why? He said He's a good fuck. I asked Is he a top? bottom? well hung? S & M? classic? Dennis answered yes to everything, but more bottom than top. I watched. I thought Well why not? As if by chance, the guy took off his T-shirt that very moment. This looked too obvious. Of course his body was a knockout. Completely shaved. Nice tits. Not a hair on his chest. I said But what's he like to fuck? More cerebral or more physical? Dennis said More cerebral. The last time I fucked him he told me Wait, he went looking for a mirror he put under him so he could see my dick up his ass. Dennis seemed to find this a turn-on and it dampened my enthusiasm. I didn't find him hot enough not to give a fuck if he was going to use me. I asked Was it with or without a condom? Without, said Dennis. I decided not to do him. It was getting too tempting.

I went to the bar for cold beers. I ran into other friends. Marcello announced he'd got his second nipple pierced. He asked And when are you going to get around to it? I said Me? Never. I'm not into nipple rings, I don't want to lose my sensitivity. Marcello asked me if I still had his phone number. I said Yes. He said Then call me some time, I still haven't forgotten when we were in Italy. I said No, me neither, and it was true. But I didn't want to call him. I found myself alone in the middle of the bar with a beer in my hand. I looked around me at my dream destroyed.

Finally I hooked up with a new thing. My height, short brown hair, very good-looking, hard body, black jeans, black T-shirt. Another star, but I had the hots for him anyway. I looked at him. He looked at me, sufficiently interested. I smiled. He smiled, his not great teeth a little spaced and pointed. It made him sexier I thought. We talked. I quickly posed the two or three essential questions. Yes he was versatile. No he wasn't into too rough S & M. OK, I said, let's go. We took a taxi. He didn't have a car, a poorboy obviously. In the taxi we did some touching. It was all right. Then we got to my place and he started putting his hands on my ass in the stairway, kind of macho, I let him do it, he put his fist between my buns to make me go up the stairs, it reminded me of Quentin, though only an approximation, a bit too rough. It made me horny in fact, a cute guy going to take me in hand for once, and not the other way around.

In the entrance hallway he started biting my neck. I don't like that at all. I backed away immediately so things would be clear. We went in. I served two scotches, I rolled a joint, we began smoking. Then we undressed, naked he was truly a paragon, we kissed, in each other's arms, I was real turned on. He began biting me again. I tensed up. He stopped. We began touching again. He bit me. I backed away. I looked at him. What do you think that's supposed to do for me, biting me like that? I said. You think it's a pleasure for me? I haven't stopped trying to show you the contrary. So what's the deal, what are you looking to get into? He said I felt like doing it that's all. He came back at me for us to start pawing at each other again. I said I think we're going to stop now. I stayed sitting at the head of the bed. He got up, he put on his black underwear, his black socks, his black jeans, his black T-shirt, his black hi-tops, in silence. I walked him to the door, still without a word.

I shut the door. I stood there without moving. I said to myself How can a thing like this be happening to me? From the window I saw him cross the courtyard. I thought This man in black is a sign. If I stay here I'm going to die. I'm going to finish up putting my semen in everybody's ass and having the same thing done to me. The truth is there's nothing I want to do any more but that. Actually it's already well under way. Of course I won't be able to speak about this to anyone. I'll no longer be able to meet anyone. I'll wait and get sick. Surely it won't last long. Then I'll be so disgusted with myself it will finally be the moment to kill myself. I told myself there was nothing left but to go away.

15 EXIT

I was lucky. I was offered a job very far away. I thought, I'm disappointed in love, I'm going away to the end of the world, it's what you have to do in a case like this. I accepted. I stayed one month more to settle business, see people, my friends, my grandmother. I wanted to leave things in order.

I phoned Terrier. I hadn't heard from him in a long time. He told me he wasn't doing anything. He was still unemployed. He was staying home all the time except weekends sometimes when he saw his mother. He wasn't going out any more. He'd had it waiting for Prince Charming. I didn't propose we see each other. I was afraid it would be too sad. He didn't propose it either. He wished me bon voyage. Said he would come see me. I said there wouldn't be any problem. I wondered if I'd pay his trip some day. Maybe.

Stéphane was my final rendezvous. He'd told me he preferred seeing me just before my departure because he was too busy before, but I'd thought the real reason was more profound, that he was thinking this goodbye was better a farewell. He was to come to get me for lunch. It was Saturday. Of course, I hadn't been able to get up on time to be ready, I'd spent the night out again. I let him in, a bathrobe scarcely pulled around me. I went and got immediately back into bed. He sat on the edge. We talked. About him, me, his new boyfriend. And then because of the emotion we went into each other's arms. Electric erection. We kissed. It was very strong. I said to him Get undressed. We were naked on the bed. I was very turned on. I told myself I was going to leave him a happy souvenir. I knelt down to his dick and I sucked him like I'd never done before. Loving it. He all but came. I got back up. I said Who fucks who? He said I'd like to fuck you, I hardly remember how it was. I agreed, I thought this was better than the other way around, in the context. It was absolutely great. After, I invited him to lunch, a brasserie in Les Halles. We drank like it was going out of style. We laughed. He drove me home. I watched him drive off, his pretty little head framed in profile in the car door. He waved before he turned back down the street. Night had fallen. I know I should have left him a lot earlier, when I told myself the first time I would never be in love with him. But his loving me was so good. It was good.